DIRT

Laura Baggaley

Habitat Press
2025

For Mina and Freya

ONE

Sam

The girl rode into town wearing a sunhat as big as a bicycle wheel.

Sam watched her pedalling the rustiest bike he had ever seen, right down the middle of the dusty road. There was something lofty about her, as if the hat were a crown. Where had she come from? The east track out of town led nowhere but the impassable Cragg Hills.

As the girl drew nearer, Sam noticed that her junk-heap bike didn't squeak or rattle as he would have expected. It glided smoothly along, the spring sunshine casting an enormous hat-shadow that slid over the ground with it.

She glanced sideways as she drew level with him, and suddenly braked.

She waited.

Sam waited too. Then he realised that she expected him to come to her. She sat perfectly still astride the bicycle, making no effort to turn or meet him halfway.

He was too curious to resist, but walked deliberately slowly to keep her waiting.

"Why aren't there any trees?" she said.

Sam stopped walking. It was a weird question.

He shrugged. "Why would there be?"

"How can there not be?"

She sounded so outraged he grew impatient.

"You can't grow trees alongside crops," he said, his tone patronising. "They'd steal water from what you're growing."

She stared at him as if he were speaking a foreign language, her expression somewhere between furious and confused. Maybe she doesn't know about farming, he thought. Then he wondered again where she could possibly have come from. Everyone knew about farming.

"Is that your family Square?" She pointed to the large area of empty earth he'd just been weeding.

"Yup."

"Why is it a rectangle?"

"Squares don't have to be square, y'know." He wrinkled his forehead. "Is it different where you come from? Where do you come from?"

He stared at her and she looked away, her eyes

squinting sideways like a kid caught doing something naughty.

"No different," she said airily. "I know all about Squares. Government land allocations. For growing on."

It sounded like she'd memorised the phrases. Sam wasn't convinced she'd ever seen a Square before, but he couldn't imagine how that was possible. Every household in the country had a Square.

He was intrigued. "So where do you come–?"

She cut off his question. "No trees at all?"

Sam paused, tempted to push for information. He decided to humour her.

"There are some on Main Street," he said, pointing. "That way."

She stared at him and he felt like an idiot. As if some foreign kid would come to Newbeck to look at scrawny trees sprouting from the pavement of the only proper street in town. But then he wasn't even sure she was foreign – her accent was exactly the same as his.

"Can you show me?" she said. "Main Street?"

It felt more like an order than a request.

Sam looked at his house. His parents were still at work – Mum at the architects' office where she worked in project planning, Dad at the solar construction factory in the next town – but it was Chores Hour for Sam and his younger brother, Casey. Sam had spent the past thirty minutes methodically walking up and down the bald dirt furrows of the Square, plucking every tiny scrap of green that had dared peek above the ground since yesterday. He'd only collected a handful of weeds. His parents probably wouldn't notice if he skipped the rest of it – Casey had most likely skimped on whatever his task was indoors.

She raised her pale eyebrows at him.

"Okay," he said.

The girl dismounted and pushed her bicycle along. She was about his height – not tall. Sam wondered how old she was. He guessed about his age – fifteen – but her confident manner made her seem older.

They walked side by side towards town. Sam's family lived on the very edge of the eastern side of Newbeck, and Main Street was about a mile away.

Their next-door neighbour, Bridget, was sweeping her porch and waved a friendly hello.

"Who's that?" the girl asked.

"Our neighbour. Bridget."

"Is she nice?"

"Uh, yeah. I guess."

Sam waved back, hoping Bridget didn't know he was meant to be doing chores, and picked up the pace a little. They walked on without speaking for a while. Then Sam looked at the silent bike. He couldn't even tell what colour it had once been – it was all-over flaking rust, held together with clamps and lumpy patches of welded metal.

"Your bike..." He trailed off, unsure how to formulate the question without rudeness.

"It's a perfectly functioning bicycle disguised as a wreck," she said, her voice tinged with pride. She didn't explain further, and Sam grew even more curious. He was about to ask another question when he was interrupted by a familiar shout from across the street.

"Oi, Rockstar!"

It was the twins.

"Who's your girlfriend?"

"Ignore them," he said quickly.

The two boys were shooting hoops in front of their house. The taller one, Caldo, had stopped marking Marley, so as to yell at Sam. Marley took the opportunity to land a perfect slam dunk, catching the basketball after a single bounce. He wheeled round and joined in the mocking.

"Rockstar! You wanna shoot a hoop to impress her?"

Caldo snickered at the idea.

The girl stared, apparently perplexed by the boys' derisive laughter. Sam quickened his pace.

"Who are they?" she asked.

"No-one."

They were past the twins' house now.

Caldo hurled a final yell after them. "Awwww! Not gonna play?"

Sam was relieved to hear the quick thud of the

basketball hitting the ground as the twins resumed their game.

"What is that game? Do you want to stop and play?"

Sam snorted. "Basketball? No. No I definitely don't want to. Stupidest game ever invented. How can you not know –?"

She looked cagey and he shrugged, still smarting from the encounter.

"Dumb game. Don't know why everyone loves it so much."

They walked on in silence for a few minutes.

"Is that your name?" she asked. "R–"

"No! That's just to annoy me."

He didn't admit it was bullying; he never had. It felt too pathetic. He tried to brush it off.

"They're only idiots from school."

"You go to school? What's it like?"

"You don't?"

She ignored the question and pressed the point. "What's it like?"

"Um, it's – it's like..." He struggled to find words, unable to imagine daily life without school. "It's just school. I can show you the building if you want? It's behind Main Street."

"Where the trees are."

"Right."

"Okay, let's look at it."

Before they reached Main Street, he turned the

familiar corner and led her along the back road to school. The playground was empty – school had finished for the day – but there was movement in some of the classrooms. A cleaner at work. Teachers preparing the next day's lessons.

"Trees!" she said, poking a finger between the tall wire netting that enclosed the grounds.

"Oh, yeah."

He had forgotten there were clusters of trees in the playground, and in lines surrounding the sports pitch.

"And you go there," she said, as if rehearsing an unusual, hypothetical thought. "Every day? With other kids? How many?"

"Er, about twenty in my class. There are seven classes."

Her eyes widened. "So many."

"Not really. It's a small town." He gestured at the deserted street. "Obviously."

She propped up her bike, took off her extraordinary hat and put her eye close to the netting.

"Now I can look at everything as if I'm inside the fence," she said, sounding pleased with the innovation.

Sam watched her surveying the grounds. She was extremely weird, but also the most interesting person he'd ever met.

"Have you really never been to school?" he asked.

She pulled away from the fence and gave him an assessing look. There was a diamond-shaped mark on her face from where she'd pressed against the wire.

He evidently passed her unspoken test. She shrugged and answered the question. "Home educated."

"Oh, wow. How does that–"

"It's not interesting. What do you study at school?"

"It's not interesting," he countered.

"Oh, but it is!" she protested, then noticed he was grinning. "Touché."

"What?"

"Touché! It's–"

She was interrupted by a gruff shout from the playground. "Oi!"

Sam tensed. "Quick, we have to go."

"What are you doing here after hours? No loitering!"

The voice was louder this time. Clifford, the school caretaker, was striding towards them.

Sam grabbed the girl's arm. "Come on!"

"Who's–?"

"Never mind! Go!"

She pushed her bike and balanced, standing on the nearside pedal. Sam ran alongside and they were away and round the corner before Clifford reached them.

"He's rather alarming," she commented, once they were out of sight.

"Do you always speak like that?" Sam asked,

before realising it might sound rude.

"Like what?"

He changed the subject quickly. "That was Clifford. He's the school caretaker."

"Caretaker?"

"He, uh, fixes things. Maintains the buildings, equipment. I dunno. Changes light bulbs? The thing is, he hates kids. Or maybe he hates the world – he's always in a terrible mood, anyway. Even the twins are scared of him."

"Oh, I see." She nodded sagely. "Please, can you tell me about school?"

Her green eyes were imploring, and as they walked towards Main Street, Sam found himself explaining about timetables and exams, and subjects like practical circular economics and sustainable industrial models and carbon management systems.

"What about poetry? Philosophy?"

"Er, yeah, a bit of poetry. In the first year. No philosophy."

"Geography?"

"Yeah, we do that."

She smiled. "Geography is my absolute favourite. Do you do cartography?"

"Carto-gro-what?"

"Maps."

"Nah."

Her smile faded. "Oh. That's sad. Maps are sublime."

"What's your name?" he asked.

"Avril."

It figured, Sam thought. A name as peculiar as her way of speaking.

He gestured to the street in front of them. "Ta-dah. Main Street."

Several bicycles, some delivery trikes and a couple of electric commercial vehicles were driving along the two-lane thoroughfare. A few shoppers drifted or bustled on the pavements on either side of the road. Spindly trees jutted from the ground at infrequent intervals.

"It's so busy!"

"Not really. You should see it on a Saturday. Your town must be tiny! Or do you live in a village or something?"

She looked evasive. "That kind of thing."

Sam followed her along the pavement. The street was the same as always, familiar and boring, but Avril stared at the window displays as if they were doorways to new worlds. There was the Library of Things (where everyone borrowed tools, appliances, stuff), the actual Library (where fewer people borrowed books), the Culture Club (where everyone got the bacterial food cultures and vitamins that were their staple diet) and the Local Fresh Depot (where there was a daily queue for fruit and veg rations).

Avril was interested in the Ready-and-Bespoke Clothes Store but even more fascinated by the

Repair Workshop, with its bold-but-accurate sign:
We Mend Anything!, the space divided into different areas for tech equipment, household appliances
and furniture. Sam watched Avril's face light up at
the sight of the specialist bike-service stall, and she
seemed equally enraptured by the hardware store and
the Community Arts Space, where painters and glass-
blowers worked alongside woodturners and potters,
rug makers and sculptors. They stood for a while at
the art studio, watching local artist Denley Emmitt,
who was working on yet another technicolour oil-
paint canvas with a ferocious scowl on his face.

They'd just reached the last shop in the row,
Creativ UpCycle (where most people in town had
their clothes refurbished), when Sam was accosted
by a familiar voice.

"Hello!"

"Oh, uh, hi, Rosie."

Sam's former childminder hurried past them,
pushing a buggy full of toys from the Library of
Things. She cast a curious glance at Avril.

"Wish I could stop to chat but I have to get home.
The Whittingstall triplets are arriving at mine in
half an hour!"

"Oh, right," Sam said.

"Wish me luck!" Rosie called over her shoulder.

"Good luck!" said Sam obediently. He watched
her go, then tapped Avril's shoulder. "Hey!"

Avril had been gazing dreamily at a colourful

tunic on display in the shop window. "Huh?"

"I have to get going."

"Why?"

"Because I'm supposed to be at home doing chores and if my parents hear I was in town I'll be in trouble!"

"Oh."

She trailed behind him pushing her bike slowly, apparently reluctant to leave.

"Those trees are pretty small," she said, looking back at Main Street. "Were they only planted recently?"

Sam shrugged. "They've always been there."

"Huh."

They walked on in silence, past the widely spaced wooden houses, each sitting next to its big Square of bald earth. It was late April, and it would soon be planting time.

As they neared the twins' house, Sam took a right turn to cut down a side street. Normally he made it a point of pride not to avoid walking on his own road, but their mocking had felt worse with Avril as a witness. She didn't question his change of direction and soon they were walking a parallel route towards home.

"What are they doing?" She pointed ahead to a scattered group of people moving slowly across a Square. They were all wearing white protective face masks and holding large canisters with spray tops.

Sam looked at the nearest house. In the window sat an elderly man, watching the activity on his land with a grey, set face.

"That's Mr Trigg's Square," Sam said. "It probably had too many weeds, so they're spraying it."

Avril stopped walking. "Spraying what?"

"Weedkiller."

"Poison?"

"No, chemicals." Sam thought about it. "Well, I guess it's poison to weeds. And you wouldn't want to breathe it in. But the ground needs to be clear. For crop plants."

"So they're... helping him? Mr Trigg?"

"Sort of." The expression on her face was making Sam feel uncomfortable. "If weeds grow on his Square, they're more likely to spread to the neighbours' Squares. So they're treating his land to protect their own."

"Treating. With poison."

"Yeah."

She set off again, pushing her bike and staring at the masked cohort as they passed. Sam had a strong feeling she wasn't saying everything she was thinking.

After a minute, she said, "What will you plant? On your Square?"

"Don't know," said Sam. "Depends what Green-Cult brings."

"What's that?"

Sam was dumbfounded. Life revolved around the

Green Cultivation Corporation. His parents spent half the winter worrying about the big spring visit of the agricultural megacorporation. Worrying whether they'd be able to afford enough soil, how much the extra fertiliser would cost and if it was worth it, whether they'd be able to buy all four of that year's crop seeds. GreenCult decided annually what would be best to plant in Newbeck each spring, and that determined the town's lives for the following year. Whether the crop was labour intensive or not. Whether it would thrive. How much it would yield. Sam still remembered the year his family could only afford to plant one crop, and how half of it failed. By January, they were so fed up with eating beetroot, they were almost glad their stores ran out. But by March they would've exchanged a whole vat of Bacterial Culture for just one root.

"What's GreenCult? You know," he managed to reply, "the agricultural company, Green Cultivation Corporation. They sell soil, seeds, crop stuff. You must know."

She looked at him from under the brim of her vast hat. "No. No, I don't."

"Their scientists decide what crops will be best for this area this year. Then they bring four selections for people to buy. It happens every spring. They're coming next Wednesday – we get the day off school."

"And they sell soil too?"

"Yeah. Of course. How else would we grow stuff?"

He was starting to think Avril was a bit stupid. Or maybe just a lot younger than she looked. She didn't seem to know even the most basic facts.

"Well, I think Squares are ridiculous."

She swung a leg over her motley bike and pushed herself along with a toe-tip on the ground. Sam walked a little faster to keep up with her coasting.

"I mean," she said, "my dad says they were meant to be temporary."

"They are."

"Temporary for fifty years! The Government should've fixed the supply chain by now."

"Yeah, but global infrastructure takes time to–" Despite their struggles, Sam's parents were firmly on the side of the Government.

She interrupted him. "Fifty years! Anyway, they already have replaced carbon-burning aviation. You see dirigibles in the sky all the time. I love dirigibles! Don't you?"

Sam had never really considered the question of modern air travel and, while he hesitated, Avril surged on.

"They're so beautiful – great airborne ships, like whales in the sky! And lighter-than-air transport is such a romantic notion, isn't it?" She gazed dreamily upwards for a moment, then returned to the argument in hand. "But why aren't they transporting food? And another thing! I've been researching SolarWind Shipping capacity – it's increased tenfold in the past decade! So why isn't food coming into the country?"

Sam didn't understand half of this, but he had revised his opinion of Avril's mental capabilities. Maybe she wasn't stupid, just ignorant of how Squares worked.

"I'll tell you why!" she went on. "Because the countries we want to import from don't want to share their crops! Why would they? They need to feed their own people first. In Spain and France and Italy and the Netherlands – and probably further afield, but I haven't done the research on that yet – their farmers have adapted successfully to global heating. They've adopted sustainable agricultural practices, maximised production and established food security policies."

"But–"

"While here, the Government tells us everyone should keep grubbing away on little patches of earth, supplementing the Fresh Rations with whatever people can manage to grow, desperately trying to stave off scurvy and diseases that shouldn't even exist anymore! And blaming this ridiculous situation on a non-existent global infrastructure challenge!"

She stopped and glared, as if Sam himself were responsible for the country's situation.

"It's not my fault!" he blurted.

"I know." Her tone was sweetly condescending.

Sam felt a wave of rage. "Look, you might know

about Europe and all their fancy policies–”

“I do! It’s my chief study focus. Travel is my main–”

“But you don’t know about Squares! You don’t even have one! And you don’t know about me or my family. So you can just stop criticising everything and go home! Wherever that is!”

Sam’s voice had become very loud. A thrumming silence followed.

Avril looked at him with stern consideration, her eyes narrow and lips compressed. Then, without saying another word, she pushed firmly on the bike pedal and sped away.

Sam watched her go. The road stretched straight ahead, carving a line between Squares and houses until town ran out and the surrounding land became scrubby desert. Avril was cycling directly towards the rocky hills. Sam knew that the road stopped at the base. There was a waterhole where he and his friends sometimes went swimming on hot days, if they could get out of working on the Squares. There were no buildings or other roads where she was heading. So where the hell did the strange girl come from?

TWO

Avril

She pedalled hard, resisting the urge to turn and see if the boy was watching her. Why hadn't she asked his name? Why had she started a dumb argument about politics? She hadn't wanted the conversation to end, but she'd made her grand exit and could hardly turn around now. Avril pedalled even faster.

Her hat strings tugged at her chin as the wind buffeted the brim. She hardly even needed the stupid thing; it wasn't summer and the sun had barely any heat in it. But then again, her pale skin could burn even in the shade. And besides, if she was honest with herself, she'd worn the hat as a kind of armour – for protection against strangers as much as the sun. Its large brim made her feel authoritative, even if her siblings did tease her about it.

Avril replayed the conversation in her head as she cycled, turning over the boy's words like a hoarder. He went to school. He knew twenty other kids! He could walk to a street with shops – Main Street. He liked geography too. Or did he? He definitely studied geography – but she couldn't remember if he actually liked it. It was frustrating, how the details were already disappearing. She'd have to ask him about geography. Next time. If there was a next time.

It took forty minutes to cycle to the waterhole. Clouds had crept overhead, and without the sun to cast sparkles on the water, the surface was grey-blue and uninviting. Avril dismounted from her bicycle and started hunting among the bushes for a place to hide it. Above her, a wide stream burbled down the craggy hillside, transforming into a waterfall at a rocky outcrop and feeding the pool with a steady curtain of water.

As she'd hoped, a cluster of wild rhododendron bushes a short distance from the waterhole provided complete cover for the bicycle. She stashed it behind them and checked it wasn't visible from any angle, before tying her hat to her back and climbing nimbly over and up the rocks at the water's edge. There was a knack to getting behind the waterfall without being drenched – she'd memorised the route long ago, but still sometimes got a wet arm or a splashed leg on the way. Today she climbed swiftly up the rocks and slid behind the wall of water, touched only by the mist of spray.

She stood for a moment on the ledge. It was one of her favourite places in the world. Her nose was just centimetres from the falling water, and she breathed in the damp fresh smell, letting her head fill with the pounding sound of it all crashing down in front of her. Reluctantly, after a few minutes, she turned and walked into the cave-tunnel behind her.

It was much easier without having to squeeze the bike through narrow passages and hairpin turns, as she'd had to do coming the other way. There had been a moment at a particularly tight corner – bike upright on its back wheel, torch between her teeth – when Avril had thought the bike would never fit, that it would be permanently wedged, forever barring the way to Town.

Town.

She'd been! She'd actually made it.

Avril pulled out her torch and walked slowly through the caves, the dips and inclines of the uneven floor as familiar as the furniture in her bedroom. She ran her fingers lightly across the rock wall. The sensation conjured the memory of her first visit to the tunnels, age five and finally big enough to walk as far as her three older siblings, finally big enough to explore the tunnels they so casually talked

about. Her sister and brothers hadn't made allow-
ances for her small legs; Natasha, Dustin and Ben
had run ahead with torches, their shouts echoing in
the scattered darkness. Avril had walked carefully,
holding tight to Fa's hand and looking around her.
The rock walls had thick folds and lines in them,
where millions of years of pressure had squeezed
one sedimentary layer into another – Avril had started a geology study project the very next day. Fa had
pointed out the key turns and forks in the tunnels,
shining a light on the markings so she'd never lose
her way. Everything had been clear and simple back
then. Before the raid. Before everything changed.

Avril emerged from the caves on the other side
of Craggy Hills into weak sunshine. The clouds
had passed so she tied her hat back on her head and
hurried down the slope into Home Valley. The multitude of fields and gardens spread out before her in
all their colourful variety. The fallow field was a deep
grassy-green, resting from crops this year, while the
grain fields showed their rich brown soil, ready for
planting. Trees grew at strategic intervals all over the
valley. Some had already blossomed and were putting all their energy into new spring leaves, but the
apple trees were still in flower and their pinky-white
blossoms shook in the breeze.

Avril assessed the scene. She needed to do some visible work by way of an alibi. The sun glinted on the large greenhouse and she could see two figures moving about inside. That would do. She jogged across the fields to join them.

The air inside was sultry. Avril's oldest sibling, Natasha, was busy planting seeds in wide flat trays and barely looked up when she came in. Uncle David was examining rows of numbers on the small screen set into the glass and gave Avril his customary friendly smile.

"Hey, Avril," he said. "Have a look – do you think the temperature settings are right?"

Avril peered at the figures and shook her head. "No. Looks like the thermostat has dropped off the network."

"I said it was too hot in here!" exclaimed Natasha. "But no-one ever listens to me!"

"I'll reboot the system and troubleshoot the sync," said Avril. "I'll double-check the soil readings at the same time."

"Thanks, whizz kid," said Uncle David. "You're my favourite fifteen-year-old in this family."

"I'm the only fifteen-year-old." Avril rolled her eyes but couldn't help smiling.

He started preparing a fresh seed tray for Natasha while Avril got to work on the screen.

"Where have you been, anyway?" said Natasha, her voice still irritated.

"Auntie Jodi wanted me to work on my engineering project," lied Avril smoothly.

"I don't see why you should put home schooling before farm work. The rest of us don't."

"That's only because you're all too old! None of you even do home ed anymore." Avril couldn't believe the unfairness.

"I still study, you know!" snapped Natasha. "It's been roasting in here for hours. The monitoring grid is your responsibility."

"I know!" Avril snapped back. "And if you shut up and let me concentrate, I'll fix it twice as quickly!"

"Hey, you two!" said Uncle David, his mild voice fractionally louder than usual. "Keep it friendly, huh?"

They worked in silence for a while, until Natasha knocked a jar off the counter and pumpkin seeds scattered across the greenhouse floor. Avril was startled by the clatter and Natasha's yell of frustration. She looked round. Natasha was on her knees picking up seeds and Avril could see tears welling in her eyes. She was about to go and help when Uncle David caught her eye and shook his head.

He knelt down beside Natasha and put his arm around her shoulder. "Hey, Nat, hey. It's okay. It's okay."

Natasha crumpled into sobs. "No it's not!"

Uncle David let her cry for a minute, then pulled

out a handkerchief and gave it to her. "Cheer up, Nat. I can't have my favourite oldest niece crying over spilled seeds. At least they're not tiny ones – could've been tomato seeds! We'd have lost half the pot! I'll have these picked up in no time."

He started gathering the pumpkin seeds in his palm and, his gaze on the floor, said quietly, "Can you tell me what's wrong?"

Natasha wiped her eyes and shrugged. "It doesn't matter. Just one of those days. Didn't sleep well."

"Everything seems worse when you're tired," he said. "You'll feel better tomorrow."

"Everything will be exactly the same tomorrow," Natasha said wearily. "I could've finished my degree by now. Every springtime, I think how much knowledge I could have. Fresh ideas. Farming innovations. And I didn't even get to the end of the first term."

Avril could feel her sister's frustration humming in the air, loud as a bee.

Natasha blew her nose and confessed, "I asked Fa again yesterday."

"What did he say?"

Avril waited for her sister to answer Uncle David's question, already knowing what the answer would be.

"He said not yet. He said we need more time to build back."

Uncle David tipped his handful of seeds into the jar. The sound was like a sssshhh. Avril wondered

what he was thinking. Fa was Uncle David's brother. Did they agree?

"Oh Nat." His voice was a sigh. "I'm sorry."

"Four years," said Natasha. "It's been four years."

The memory flared in Avril's mind.

The night of the raid, strangers had swarmed
the valley. They had powered along the driveway
with trucks and tools and machines, intending to
strip the fields of all the hard-grown crops. They'd
plundered the ground, flashlights taped to baseball
caps, ripping vegetables from stems and vines and
soil, tearing branches from trunks in their hurry
to collect the fruit. Most of the planting had been
destroyed as a result – trees and shrubs knocked
down by clumsy trucks, whole beds of produce
crushed by heavy wheels. And what the stupid,
greedy raiders didn't take, they wrecked.

Fa had tried to stop them. He still had the scar,
a raised line across his skull, where they'd knocked
him unconscious.

The next day Fa had blocked off the driveway.
He'd taken down the welcome sign and dragged
a fallen tree trunk across the road. Branches and
brambles heaped over the trunk made it look as if
the way was completely impassable. Every couple
of months, when supplies were needed, Fa used the

tractor to drag the barrier aside, making a gap just wide enough for the small car to pass through. He never took anyone with him. The days of trips and outings were over.

Before the raid, they had left the valley sometimes. Not often, but the world beyond was part of normal life. Occasional supply trips. The annual summer fair in the village where distant cousins lived. City visits and weekends at a holiday camp by a lake. The last drive had been to see Natasha at university, before the raid and her summons home.

Now, the furthest the cousins and siblings went was to the waterhole for swimming. They chose times when it was usually deserted: early dawn or the end of long, hot harvest days. In high summer, though, they would sometimes listen through the waterfall to the sounds of shouts and splashes. Then the whisper would go back – "Townids! Townids!" – and they'd troop home through the cool, dark caves, disappointed of their swim. No-one remembered which of them had first misheard "Town kids" as "Townids" but the name had stuck.

Natasha stood up and took the jar in her hand, resuming the task of planting pumpkin seeds, a bleak expression on her face. Uncle David squeezed her shoulder and continued prepping seed trays.

Avril returned to the screen, mechanically working step by step to troubleshoot the complex monitoring system. As she'd expected, it was a minor glitch with an easy fix, and she let her mind wander as she navigated.

Inevitably, her thoughts circled back to the boy. The Townid boy with thoughtful eyes and smooth brown skin, a colour somewhere between an acorn and a conker.

She wished she knew his name. He had seemed so clever and so stupid at the same time! His earnest belief that you should farm without trees was daft. But then he knew about school and town and economics. And the way he'd looked at her... as if she were fascinating. It had made her self-conscious and her skin had kind of prickled under the attention, but it felt good. Exciting.

Avril couldn't remember the last time someone had properly looked at her. Everyone was always too busy. Ma and Fa and her siblings were constantly in the fields or doing all the epic planning for crop-planting and field rotations. A whole wall of the family kitchen was coated in wipe-clean paint, and served as a giant noticeboard, covered in diagrams and schedules and monthly/weekly/daily tasks.

Uncle David and his wife Nessa were lovely, but they didn't really have time for Avril between farm work and children. Their kids, Christo and Lexie, were at the demanding ages of five and three – small, exhausting bombs of energy. Ma's sister, Aunt Jodi, pretended to pay attention to her, but Avril could always tell when her mind was drifting. Jodi had spent the past twenty years home-educating Avril's three siblings and her own four sons, and had pretty much run out of steam by the time Avril came along.

But the Townid boy. He had listened. He had asked questions too – questions she hadn't been able to answer.

Natasha's complaint echoed in her head: four years. They'd been in hiding for so long it had stopped feeling temporary, but until recently Avril had still believed Fa's refrain: It's only for a short time, while we build back.

It was this month that she'd lost hope. When the Easter Country Show came and went for the fourth time without anyone suggesting they attend, Avril had started planning. Fa was never going to let them leave the valley. She'd begun restoring the wrecked bike.

And today she'd made it. She'd been to Town!

Avril's thoughts were interrupted by Uncle David. "Think I'm done." He brushed soil from his fingers. "Enough trays there for you, Nat?"

"Mmm." Natasha nodded. "Thanks."

"Okay. I'm going to help Ben mulch the orchard," he said. "See you later."

He closed the greenhouse door quietly behind him. Avril half expected Natasha to pick a fight, but she seemed lost in thought. Just in case, Avril raced to restore the tech system so she could get away before another argument.

"Temperature should regulate now, Nat," she said after another ten minutes, dimming the screen. "I'm going to get a snack."

"Okay," said Natasha, then added a muted after-thought, "Thanks."

Avril left the greenhouse, skirted the orchard, where Uncle David was working with her youngest brother, Ben, and followed the hedgerow around the back of her aunts' and uncles' houses nearby. She kept herself hidden, wanting to avoid Aunt Jodi since she hadn't actually done any work on the current home education project that day. Fortunately, the hedge was tall and thick, a dense mixture of hawthorn, blackthorn, hazel and maple, so she didn't have to stoop as she hurried along. She could hear the smallest cousins, Christo and Lexie, yelling in the garden and a cloud of sparrows rose into the air, chirruping loudly. Avril walked on, crossing two small fields, and reached the family farmhouse. It was so ordinary – a big old wooden building, solar-panelled roof, cluttered veranda at the front, heat pump and rainwater-collection units along the side. If it hadn't felt like a prison, she would've loved it.

Avril took off her hat and swung it casually by the strings as she entered the kitchen. Her mother was standing on a stool, writing a new list of tasks at the top of the wall.

"Hey, Ma," said Avril.

"Oh, hi, love. What've you been doing? Anything I can tick off today's list?"

"Uh." Avril skimmed the daily bullet points. "I was sorting the heating in the greenhouse – system glitch. But it's not on the list. I'll do some weeding in a minute. Just came in for a snack."

"Hmm." Ma frowned at the notes she was writing. "Okay. I thought you might still be working on that bike you were trying to salvage the other day. Any joy with that?"

"No, uh-uh." Avril hid her face in the pantry. "I couldn't get the chain to work. Lost cause." She took a handful of dried apple rings from the big jar on the shelf.

"Ah, that's a shame." Ma climbed off the stool and stood back to look at the wall.

The front door swung open and Fa strode in holding two large mugs.

"More tea, Sophie?" He plonked the mugs on the counter and took the lid off the kettle.

"Not for me, thanks," said Ma. "I'm heading back into the garden now."

"I'll see you out there," said Fa. "What about you, Avril? Tea for me, tea for thee?"

It was one of Fa's ancient jokes, his tea rhyme, and so familiar that Avril smiled automatically.

"Yeah, thanks."

Fa topped up the kettle and switched it on. "Had a good morning?"

"Uh-huh. Upper fields, greenhouse, off to do some weeding in a minute."

"Good girl."

Avril leaned against the kitchen table and chewed an apple ring. She felt a tinge of guilt at lying, but stronger was the feeling of relief that she'd got away with it. She'd been to town and back without being caught. She'd met a Townid and nothing bad had happened.

She couldn't wait to return.

Two days later, Avril woke tingling with an almost Christmassy excitement. GreenCult Day. She just had to make it to town.

The family were gathered around the big kitchen table at breakfast, eating porridge with jam and gently bickering over the allocation of tasks for the day.

Avril's oldest siblings, Natasha and Dustin, had called dibs on the electric vehicles – the quad bike and tractor – for their jobs, and her 19-year-old brother Ben was doing a day's tree-grafting training with Uncle Frank. Ma and Fa were both going to be busy preparing the root-crop gardens for planting.

Avril scanned the wall and noticed a new bullet point. "Shall I mend the fence at the far field?" she said, going for a nonchalant tone. "Then I really ought to do some study. Auntie Jodi's on my case to finish this geography project."

"Uh-hmm," Fa agreed absently, reading the news on a handscreen.

"You still studying, nerdlet?" teased Ben.

"Unlike you, empty-brain, I actually like books." Avril pierced him with a stare. "And study. And expanding my mind."

"Quite right," said Ma. "Reading is very important. But could you also check the soft fruit cages while you've got the toolbox out, make sure the frames have survived the winter. And have a look at the bean trellises, oh, and that wobbly bit of plank–"

"Geography project, Ma!"

"Yes, just a few small tasks first. Please!"

"Fine!"

Avril bolted the last of her breakfast and was first to leave the table.

Toolbox in tow, she hurried through the tasks, made a quick stop at the greenhouse, and was soon at the far field, completing the fence-mending with a final few nails. She normally found it satisfying to mend or make things, but today she didn't stop to admire her work. Instead, she scanned the valley, confirming that no-one was nearby. She tucked the toolbox under the stile – she'd pick it up on her way home – and ran in the direction of the caves.

The Townid Boy wasn't in his Square. He wasn't anywhere to be seen.

She had assumed he would be there and now felt utterly foolish. Why had she expected him to spend every minute in the same spot outside his house? How idiotic! Then she felt almost sick with nerves. It had been easy, braving town with him beside her. It was another matter to cycle along the streets alone. She had left her biggest hat behind, and was instead wearing a small cap with a visor to shade her face, but she still felt self-conscious. What if people looked at her? She wasn't used to strangers.

She dismounted and pushed her bike slowly along in front of the boy's house, uncertain about continuing. She was almost ready to turn around and cycle back to the waterhole when she heard loud noises in the distance – a strange combination of machinery and voices, like nothing she'd heard before. Avril was too curious to resist. She took a deep breath and cycled towards the sound.

At first sight, it looked like an army had arrived in town. Black-clad security guards stood to attention, accompanying a convoy of enormous trucks that seemed to stretch for ever. Each vehicle was as wide as the road itself and rolled slowly forward on fat caterpillar tracks. The truck bodies were made of curved, shiny black metal and seemed to have legs along their sides that scuttled in the air like an upturned beetle's. Crowds of onlookers had gathered in front of the houses and Squares on either side and were jostling and calling out to the operators as they worked. Avril had never seen so many people, and she'd certainly never seen anything like these trucks.

The torso of the nearest vehicle was split open along the spine, as if it had opened its wings. Watching carefully, Avril realised that the legs were sets of hydraulic arms, tipped with buckets, that were reaching inside the truck body and lifting something down to the ground. But what were they shifting? She craned her neck but couldn't see for people. Most of the crowd were simply watching, enjoying the spectacle of ten vast trucks and their regiment of workers, but some were agitated, trying to make themselves heard over the noise of machinery and the chattering of their neighbours, with shouts of "But it's my turn!" and "You've missed my Square!"

No-one seemed interested in Avril. Heart thudding, she dismounted and left the bicycle lying on the edge of the road. She crept towards the throng and, standing a short distance away, craned her neck to discover the focus of the gathering.

The huge bucket on the nearest truck arm

swung sideways, and Avril watched the contents tip in a brown muddy waterfall onto the Square at the roadside.

Soil.

Avril blinked in confusion. People were tussling to buy soil.

"Hello."

She jumped. It was the boy.

"Hello," she said.

There was an awkward silence. She couldn't tell what he was thinking behind those conker-brown eyes, and wondered if he was still angry with her.

She asked quickly, so she didn't forget this time, "What's your name?"

"Sam."

"Hi, Sam."

She might have imagined it, but it seemed like his expression softened a little.

After another pause, he spoke. "So, you came to see GreenCult day." He gestured to the activity behind him.

"Yeah, had some free time, so..." She tried to sound casual, but couldn't help blurting the question at the front of her brain. "What are they doing?"

"They're delivering the soil and seeds for the year." He looked back at the milling swarm. "Everyone always goes a bit crazy on GreenCult day. It's silly really. They never actually miss a Square, or leave anyone out, but it's so chaotic it always feels like they could. So, people get pushy, trying to make sure their Square gets served first."

"Has yours been done?"

"No. Being at the end of the road means sometimes we're first, sometimes we're last. They started at another street this year so today we're–"

"Last?" She finished the sentence for him.

"Right!"

Avril's head was knotted with so many questions she couldn't untangle the right one to ask, and she found herself distracted by how perfectly symmetrical Sam's ears were.

"Where's your hat?" He gestured to her little cap.

"Oh, uh, um. At home." She felt herself turning a little pink – it was an unfamiliar experience, being lost for words.

"So you do have a home!" Sam's voice was teasing. "I thought maybe you were an apparition from the peaks of Craggy Hills, from another dimension beyond–"

"I look human, don't I?" She cut him off quickly, not wanting to talk about the geography of home, even in a joke.

"Oh yes. Definitely."

He glanced round. The convoy was edging towards them, its progress slow but implacable.

"We should move your bike," he said. "Don't want it to get crushed."

"Oh! Yes."

"Shall we go up the road, wait at my Square for the delivery?"

Avril looked at the extraordinary scene. Part of her wanted to stay and watch the spectacle – there were more people than she'd ever seen in one place in her life, and strange machines operating on a vast scale – but she had so much to ask him.

"Sure." She retrieved her bike and walked alongside Sam towards his house. It was easier to think with the noise and hustle fading behind them.

"So this is the annual visit?"

"Yup."

"I saw the soil. What about the seeds?"

"Yeah, the AgriCarriers bring both. Seeds are at the front of the vehicles. You have to take your containers to be filled at the chutes."

"Oh, I see. And they decide what you buy?"

"Yeah, their scientists make the selection. They do long-range weather forecasts and analysis of the new soil and all that sort of thing." Sam grinned. "Hey! This year is a good one – my parents are getting sweetcorn, cabbages and broccoli."

"That's all?"

"It's three! Four is the maximum and we can't afford them all. Last year we only had two. And these are actually tasty, better than, I dunno... better than beetroot!"

He seemed so pleased; she didn't know what to say. They walked on in silence for a moment, while questions buzzed louder and louder in her head. She didn't want to start another argument, but she had to know.

Tentatively, she asked, "Why do you buy soil? Don't you have any?"

He looked perplexed. "Well, yeah, I mean we have last year's. But it's exhausted from crop-growing. You can't just keep planting in the same soil, there wouldn't be any nutrients left."

He glanced at her, perhaps expecting a reply, but she kept her mouth shut.

Sam's house was the same as all the others: a square, wood-frame building bleached grey by the sun, roofed with winking solar panels and guarded by a single tall wind turbine standing sentinel against the wall. It had a small porch and four steps leading up to the yellow front door.

Sam perched on the top step and invited Avril to join him. The step was wide enough for them to sit side by side without touching, but she could sense the warmth of his shoulder through her tunic and felt conscious that their knees were only centimetres apart.

They watched the convoy moving along the road towards them, the unceasing arms pouring and throwing soil onto different areas of the Squares on either side. Avril saw people holding buckets to be filled, seeds pouring from tubes that protruded at the front of the AgriCarriers like so many antennae.

"Oh!" she remembered. "I brought you something."

She took the light hemp knapsack off her shoulders and cradled it carefully on her lap, gently unfolding the fabric and lifting something out. With her hands occupied, it was easier to say the few words she'd planned.

"Um, kind of an apology." She opened the parcel, focusing all her attention on it. "For being argumentative."

On her knees, wrapped in straw and paper, were six little seedlings.

Sam stared at the green shoots as if she'd performed a magic trick. "Where did you get them?"

Avril ignored the question and pointed at the tender leaves. "These three are strawberry plants, these are tomatoes." She was almost certain Natasha wouldn't notice the small gaps in the greenhouse rows at home.

"They need to be kept indoors a bit longer. You can plant them out when it gets warmer."

She placed the bundle into Sam's cupped hands, and he received the seedlings as carefully as if they were a kitten that might jump away. He stared at her gift intently.

"Thank you," he said. "Avril, how did you –?"

She jumped up. "Look! They're nearly at your Square!"

Her interruption was only a slight exaggeration.

The crowd was certainly getting closer, and Avril could feel more than one pair of eyes looking at her. Sam replaced the straw around the seedlings and re-rolled the paper.

"Hang on," he said, jumping up and going inside.

Avril hopped off the steps and grabbed her bike, then hurried along the edge of Sam's Square, away from the multitude accompanying the AgriCarriers.

It took Sam a few slow minutes to catch up. He must've been hiding the seedlings indoors, as he was now empty-handed. His gait was slightly lopsided, a lollop rather than a jog. It struck Avril as uniquely endearing.

"Hey," he said, a little out of breath.

"Hey."

They stood and watched the beetle machines finish the neighbours' Square. Avril saw how the first truck tipped its load along the nearest strip of Square, while the second and third used their hydraulic arms to fling soil across the farthest areas of the patch of earth. At the edge of the crowd she noticed a couple, a bit younger than her parents, standing with tubs and buckets at the front of the AgriCarrier. The man had close-cropped black hair and light brown skin, an older version of Sam.

"Is that your dad?" she asked.

"Yup. And my mum. And younger brother. Casey."

His parents were smiling as they tapped the

paychip to the truck dispenser. Each held up containers to catch the flow of seeds. Casey, a lanky kid, held up a bucket to the third tube.

"I should be helping them," he said. "Stay here?"

"Okay."

Avril watched him run over and speak to his parents. Sam and his brother carted the three seed tubs between them back to the house and took them inside. While she waited for him to reappear, Avril sidled closer to the nearest AgriCarrier, fascinated by the movement of the robotic arms. A short guard with a dark moustache was on duty at the front of the vehicle, looking bored. Avril moved to stand next to him.

"Do you use remote controls?" she said. "For the hydraulic arms? Or are they automated?"

The man stared at her, a surprised expression on his face. She waited for a reply, then when he didn't speak, added, "I'm interested in automotive engineering. Dirigibles are my passion, but the mechanics of these AgriCarriers are fascinating."

His moustache twitched and his mouth formed the suspicion of a smile.

"Automated," he said, then jerked his head. "You'd better move away. I'm not supposed to chat."

"Oh, shame. Thanks anyway."

Avril wandered to the edge of Sam's Square. When she glanced back at the guard, he gave her a wink and she smiled. A moment later, Sam emerged from the yellow front door of his house. Instead of returning to the crowd, he turned towards Avril and ran with his loping stride to join her.

"Hi." He grinned.

"Hi." She found herself smiling back. "So, your brother's the tall one?"

Sam groaned. "Yep. Taller than me. Faster. Good at basketball."

"The hoop sport everyone's obsessed with?" Avril remembered the twins and their mocking.

"Yeah."

"Stupid game," she pronounced.

Sam looked sideways at her and she hoped he got it – she was putting down the bullies, not his brother. She felt uncertain and changed the subject.

"Casey, huh? Where's he gone?"

"He's gonna watch the soil-spreading from his bedroom window. My parents told him to keep an eye, check we're not short-changed. Dunno what they think we'd do if GreenCult did under-deliver. I mean, those guards hardly look like they'd welcome complaints, right?"

Avril looked at the security contingent surrounding the trucks and realised they were all carrying batons and wearing vests that looked suspiciously like body armour.

"Why do they even need security?" she asked. "Do people cause trouble?"

Sam shook his head. "Not here, not in Newbeck.

But I guess it happens some places. This stuff is valuable. Can you think of anything more valuable than soil?"

"I guess not."

The vehicles had reached Sam's family property and he whooped.

"Here we go!"

The trucks' arms poured and tipped and threw and hurled, until the Square of earth was like a messy painting, black new soil splattered and scattered across the old grey dirt.

An electronic whistle sounded, signalling the final delivery. The hydraulic arms immediately retracted, the body-containers closed, and the trucks picked up speed. The security guards jumped onto ledges set along the sides, gripping hand-brackets and staring straight ahead from within their black helmets. The crowd of onlookers stopped following and gathered in the road, waving and whooping as the convoy whirred away into the desert. The huge machines were quiet now their beetle-legs were tucked away, buckets no longer scraping and banging; the electric motors spun silently as they passed Avril and Sam.

They seemed to be heading directly for the waterhole, and Avril thought for a mad moment that the AgriCarriers would circle Cragg Hills and suddenly turn up at Home Valley. But then the leading truck swung off the road, forging its own track due north across the flat desert, vehicular comrades following like ants in a line. When they were small as a string of black beads, the townspeople began to disperse, nattering among themselves about the day's events. Only a few of them spared a glance for the stranger at the end of the last Square, but Avril kept her distance until the street had cleared, nervous of possible questions.

Once the last people had left, Avril crouched down by Sam's Square and picked up a handful of soil. She squeezed it with her fingers, pressing it into the palm of her hand. When she looked up, Sam was watching her.

"Is this... good soil?" she asked.

"The best," said Sam. "GreenCult only sells top-of-the-range products. Of course, things grow much better if you can afford the fertiliser as well, but we can't. Not this year."

"Sam!" called an adult voice from the distance. "Sam!"

"That's my mum," said Sam. "Probably wants me to start raking straight away."

"I've got to go too," said Avril, letting the handful of earth fall back to the ground. She dusted her grubby palm on her trousers and picked up her bike.

"See you – ?"

"Yeah, see you – sometime," she replied. "Soon."

THREE

Sam

"Where did you get them?" Sam's mum had an expression on her face he'd never seen before, a confused mixture of anger and doubt and suspicion.

"I've told you!" He was furious that she didn't trust him. "A friend gave them to me!"

"That doesn't make sense, Sam! Strawberries and tomatoes aren't selected crops this year. They haven't been selected crops since before you were born!"

"Not a friend that you know. A friend from out of town." He met her gaze, stare for stare.

"How can you have a friend from out of town? What on earth –?"

"A girl. Avril. She was here on GreenCult day."

"That girl with the bicycle? But where did she come from?"

"I don't know!"

"What do you mean, you don't know? She must come from somewhere!"

"She didn't say!"

"Lily, what's going on?" Dad appeared at the top of the porch steps.

Mum turned round and reached out a hand. "Dexter, look at this."

Dad walked down the steps and took her hand. Sam stood defiantly at the edge of the Square, arms folded, and said nothing.

Dad stared at the small plants forming a tiny row in the earth. "What are these?"

"Strawberries and tomatoes," said Sam. "The forecast is warmer, so I've planted them out."

"I don't mean what type of plants! I mean where did they come from? Seedlings don't appear out of thin air!"

"That's what I've been asking him!" Mum cut in.

Dad's voice was careful. "Have you been stealing?"

"No!"

Sam stormed past his parents. He slammed the front door behind him, took the stairs two at a time and slammed his bedroom door for good measure.

His parents' voices floated up to him.

"Leave him to calm down."

"I'm so worried..."

He shut them out by playing his latest track at high volume. The complex guitar solo and heavy drums thrummed in his ears, outracing his furious pulse until he felt less enraged.

Gradually, Sam became distracted by the need to tweak the balance. He woke the familiar software on his deskscreen, watching the music waves as he listened and contemplating whether the track needed another element to complete it. As he began playing around with the different components, absorbed by the challenge of perfecting the music, Sam completely forgot about the little plants causing a ruckus below.

"Hi," said Avril.

She was smiling at him, and he found himself smiling back, despite the trouble her plants had caused.

"Hi," he said.

They were on the desert road, partway between his house and the waterhole. Sam had been in his bedroom, playing guitar, when he saw Avril's bicycle approaching in the far distance, her pink sunhat vivid against the beige landscape. He had run downstairs immediately and cycled out to warn her about his parents. For the past two days, Mum and Dad had continued to interrogate him about the seedlings, until Sam had given in and promised to introduce them to his "out-of-town friend" the next time he saw her.

She stopped when he drew near and waited for his approach, smiling at him from under the bright brim of her hat. He pulled up and raised a hand in greeting, failed to find words to tell her about his parents and gestured to Avril's bike instead.

"What's that?"

Attached with ropes to the back was a shallow wooden box mounted on a mismatched set of wheels. It had a piece of sacking tied over it.

"It's a... I don't know what you'd call it. A miniature trolley? Or a wheeled sled, maybe? I made it. I was in a bit of a hurry. Construction is usually my thing – I just didn't have much time." Her pale cheeks were tinged pink, and she had a sweaty glow on her forehead from pulling the extra load.

"But – but what's it for? What's in it?" said Sam.

"I wanted to show you something. I was going to bring it to your Square."

"Is it more seedlings? Because they kinda–"

"No! No, sorry, I can't bring more of those. I'd get in trouble."

Sam frowned.

"I didn't steal them or anything," Avril added quickly, much to his relief. "Just – it's complicated."

They looked at each other for a moment. Sam had so many questions, but he was still smarting from his parents' distrust and didn't want to make

Avril feel like he doubted her.

"Shall we swap bikes for the rest of the way?" he said, offering his handlebars. "That looks heavy."

"It's not so bad," she said, "But yeah, that'd be good."

They swapped bikes and cycled alongside one another on the packed-earth road. Sam could feel the drag of the trolley behind him, the weight lurching a little as it pulled on its tethers, but the bike itself was a much smoother ride than his own. He glanced at Avril – what did she make of his rattling gears and squeaky wheels?

As if she'd heard his thoughts, she said, "You got a toolbox at home? I'll take a spanner to your brake bolts if you like. They're a bit loose."

He gave an embarrassed shrug. "Thanks, um, maybe. I've been meaning to... You know, been busy... since GreenCult day."

"Yeah!" She nodded recognition. "Life in spring-time, huh? Never-ending tasks."

"Uh-huh."

"Nearly couldn't get away today, but I–" She stopped and bit her lip.

Sam wondered what she'd been going to say. She was always so secretive, he thought. He gave an inner groan at the thought of his parents quizzing her. He had to prepare her.

"So, uh, my parents kind of want to meet you."

She looked at him and her green eyes were huge.

Suddenly realising how it sounded, he blurted, "Because of the seedlings."

"Oh."

"I mean, they like them…"

"Oh, good."

"They just want to meet you."

The explanation felt glaringly incomplete, but Sam couldn't bring himself to utter the rest of the sentence: because they think you or I or both of us are plant thieves and they're demanding to know where the seedlings you gave us came from…

Feeling like a coward, he kept pedalling.

"It would be nice to meet them," she said, sounding as if she was choosing her words carefully. "I can't be out for long today, need to get back. You know, springtime chores and all that."

"Yeah, sure. Of course."

Out of the corner of his eye, he could see her long white fingers gripping the handlebars as she pedalled his bike. The short fingernails had a thin line of dirt caught under them, like his own and everyone else's at this time of year, and there was an oil smudge across her knuckles, but Avril's hands somehow looked as elegant as if she were a pianist or a painter. He had a strange urge to kiss her wrist and looked away quickly.

They were approaching the edge of town. To Sam's relief, none of his family was outside the house. He and Avril dismounted at the farthest end of their

Square. He hoped no-one was looking out of the window. Avril was already busy untying the sacking cover, revealing the contents of the small sled.

"Look!" she said, with some pride. "Feel it!"

The shallow box was full of soil. Sam crouched beside it and took a handful in his palm. Avril bent over the family land and lifted a handful of recently delivered GreenCult soil. She brought it over and thrust it into his other hand.

"Here!" Her eyes were solemn and urgent. "Can you see?"

Sam stood up, examining the two fistfuls he held. They were completely different. As usual, the soil from his Square was dry and gritty, almost chalky, and peppered with little stones. Bits of it fell from between his fingers like sand. Avril's soil was soft and squashy. He squeezed and it formed a loose ball. There were no stones and, as he examined it, something wriggled across his thumb.

"A worm!"

"Worms are a sign of good soil." Avril touched her hand to his and let the worm crawl onto her palm.

"I know!" Sam's parents always got excited if they found a worm in the Square.

Their cupped hands hovered together in the air, thumbs pressing against each other, as the little creature inched across. Sam usually thought worms were a bit gross, but all he could think about was the warm pressure of Avril's thumb against his, and the fact that her head was so close to his that her long hair was touching his shoulder.

"Sam!"

Mum's voice broke the spell.

"Sam!"

Avril stepped away and delivered the worm to the safety of the soil box. Sam's parents were hurrying towards them.

"Sorry," said Sam. "Those are my parents. Like I said..."

"They want to meet me?" Avril sounded freaked.

"Yeah, I'm really sorry. They're just... really... curious people..."

She knelt and untied the trolley from her bike, fumbling with knots that had been pulled tight as it dragged, muttering under her breath until it came free. Sam's folks were getting closer. Avril wheeled the trolley towards the Square.

"This is for you," she said. "It's only a tiny amount – it's all I could carry – it won't make any difference. I just–"

"Hello!" called Mum as they covered the last few metres of ground. "You must be Avril. Hello." She was panting slightly from half-jogging the whole length of the Square, and her face was fixed in a fake-welcome smile.

"Hi." Avril's voice was tiny.

"I'm Dexter and this is Lily." Dad grabbed her hand and pumped it up and down, also wearing a determinedly social grin. "It's so nice to meet you."

There was a hideous silence. Avril gave Sam an imploring look and his brain panic-searched for words but failed.

"So, uh," Avril whispered. "I need to be going–"

"What's this?" asked Mum, looking at the box on wheels.

Sam found his voice. "Avril brought us some soil. Isn't that nice of her?" He hoped his voice conveyed the intended message to his parents: Don't accuse her of stealing!

Dad was already kneeling by the trolley and lifting a handful of the contents.

"This is... this is the best soil I've ever seen," he said quietly. "This is like nothing I've ever... Where does it come from?"

"Oh, uh, just – just my family's land," said Avril, her voice sounding as tense as Sam was feeling. "Anyway, I really need to–"

"From GreenCult?" said Dad, standing up and staring at her.

"Where do you live?" asked Mum. "What's your family name? Where do you come from?"

"Nowhere!" Avril's voice sliced through the questions, and Sam could see alarm in her eyes. "Look, I'm not even into farming!"

She was almost yelling.

"What?" Dad looked confused.

"My whole family are crazy for farming and I'm

not even that interested! I just wanted to show you what good soil really looks like. Because Sam said GreenCult's was the best." Avril swung a leg over her bike. "But it's barely even soil. They're selling you dirt!"

"Wait, please–" Dad took a step towards her.

"I have to go." Avril pushed off and began cycling swiftly away. "Bye, Sam."

"Bye," he called, feeling helpless.

"GreenCult is fooling everyone!" she shouted over her shoulder, then pedalled even faster. Soon her hat was a small pink splodge in the distance.

FOUR

Avril

By the time she reached the waterhole, Avril was breathless and sweating from cycling so fast. She'd kept glancing behind her all the way, and even though she knew she wasn't being followed, her body was as full of adrenaline as if she were being chased.

How could she be so stupid? Of course Sam's parents were going to ask questions! Especially since they lived in a town where everyone thought it was normal to buy terrible soil and grow only four crops!

Avril shoved the bicycle behind the bush, pulled off her shoes and sat on a rock to plunge her feet in the pool. The cold water sharpened her thoughts, and she leaned down to dip in her forearms and splash her hot face. It felt so good that she dipped her hat in the water, shook it a bit, then put it on her head. The drips ran down her face and hair, wetting the back of her tunic and cooling her skin.

She tried to think straight. If her parents found out she'd spoken to not one but three town people, she'd never be allowed out of their sight again. Fa's voice echoed in her head: "If they find us, our lives will be destroyed. Remember the raid."

And she did remember. It had been terrifying. Helping Ma and her siblings barricade the bedroom door with furniture, then hiding under the covers of her parents' bed as the night air filled with sounds of destruction.

But that was four years ago. The fields and gardens were back to their flourishing selves and the raiders had never returned. They couldn't spend the rest of their lives in hiding!

Even as she thought this, Avril heard Fa's voice again, relentlessly drumming his message home. "Never go past the waterhole. Never talk to town people. Don't trust anyone."

Living in hiding was exactly what he wanted. If her parents found out she'd aroused suspicion in three town people she'd never be allowed to leave the house again. Solution: make sure her parents never got to know about it. Keep away from Town. Simple. After all, she'd been there now. She'd fulfilled her ambition and that was that.

Feeling decisive, Avril shook the water from her feet and put her shoes on. Time to go home.

Avril spent the next week trying to go back to normal life. She did all her farm chores with extra commitment and started an upcycling project, building a retractable storage system for tools in the greenhouse. She bickered with her siblings and avoided going up to the far fields that led to the caves.

But Sam's face kept popping into her head. He'd looked so guilty when his parents tried to question her – she knew it wasn't his fault. If anything, she blamed herself for offering gifts that so clumsily advertised her existence to them. What had she been thinking? Avril cringed with embarrassment at the thought. Who gives presents to someone they've only just met? And what boy wants a rickety box full of soil from some weird girl they probably don't even like?

She tried not to think about it. Yet she couldn't help remembering the way it had felt when they'd stood with their hands pressed together, looking at that palmful of soil. Sam's thumb had moved against hers, in an infinitesimal caress, and she could swear she'd felt his soft breath on her shoulder. Vivid images would appear in her mind at odd moments – when she was digging and saw a worm, or smelled the soil, or for no reason at all – Sam's eyes, the touch of his hand, his smile or his ears or the way he said "Hi".

And so, her firm decision never to go to Town again started to melt. No Town meant no Sam, and that felt simply impossible.

She began to argue with herself. It must be possible to see Sam and avoid his parents. The day she first met him, a Monday, he'd said his parents were at work. So, if she went on a Monday at the same time as before, Sam would be at home for chores and his parents would be out. That would be fine, surely?

Sam's Square was deserted. Avril had cycled hard from the waterhole, feeling painfully conspicuous the whole way. She was wearing dusty beige clothes and a khaki cap in the faint hope of blending into the desert area between the edge of town and the hills, but a lone cyclist on an empty road was bound to stand out in an otherwise motionless landscape. She wished there were trees to hide behind.

Avril left her bicycle lying at the side of the road and cautiously approached the house. It was a bright afternoon in early May, the sunshine burnishing the windows like shields. Impossible to tell if anyone was inside. She sidled along the wall and peeped through the big window that stretched alongside the porch. The front room was empty. She stood still, leaning against the warm wood, and tried to figure out what to do.

Then she heard it.

Music. Someone was playing a guitar above her head. Her thoughts raced. The person was playing fast. Notes rippled in the air, flowing swift as a mountain stream. Could it be Sam? What if it was one of his parents? Or his brother?

But it could be Sam.

Avril ran to the Square. The seedlings were bigger already, packed around with the soil she'd brought – a fertile little patch in the expanse of thin earth. Avril avoided the plants and rummaged in a bit of GreenCult soil, immediately finding what she needed. She took the handful of pebbles to the front of the house and looked up at the first-floor window. Ready to run if it wasn't him, she lobbed the stones up at the glass. The beautiful melody stopped and the window was pushed open.

"Sam!"

"Avril!"

He looked so pleased to see her that her spine tingled. He was holding a guitar.

"Wait there! I'll come down."

In a moment he was at the door. "Do you want to come in?"

Avril hesitated.

"I'm the only one home. Mum and Dad are at work and Casey's gone to play basketball."

"Alright."

She climbed the steps and followed him inside.

The hallway was dim and cool after the bright sunshine outdoors. The walls had even better insulation than at home. Sam led the way upstairs. Avril followed slowly, taking in the family photos on the wall and peering through the open doorways on the landing. She'd never been in a stranger's house before and was hungry to know how other people lived.

Sam's parents' bedroom was plain and sparse, containing a cream double bed and a tall grey wardrobe. The curtains were cream too, as if the room wanted to be as quiet as possible. It couldn't be more different from the clashing patchwork quilt and clutter that filled her parents' room at home. A box room to the left was only just big enough for its single bed, and the walls were busy with basketball posters.

"Uh, come in?" Sam said, holding open a door on the right of the landing.

Avril blushed, belatedly realising she might seem nosy.

"Er, sorry," she said, crossing past the top of the stairs and following Sam into his bedroom. She stood just inside the doorway while he pulled a blanket over rumpled bedsheets and kicked some clothes from the floor under the desk.

"Sorry," he said, removing a guitar from the chair by the desk. "Have a seat."

She perched on the chair and discovered to her delight that it swivelled. Sam sat on the bed and laid the guitar beside him.

"That was you playing, wasn't it?" Avril asked, twisting the chair from side to side as she sat.

"Oh, er, yes."

"You're really good."

"Thanks. Not really. Not as good as I want to be."

"Is your family musical then?"

Sam laughed. "Nope! Not at all. My parents are tone deaf and Casey's only interested in sport. Apparently, there was a great-uncle who was in a band, maybe I get it from him."

"Are you in a band?"

He shook his head regretfully. "I wish. Our school's too small to have more than one specialist teacher. We've got a PE teacher but no-one to teach music."

"How did you learn then?"

"First from videos. Then from a guy at the Community Art Space in town. He was mainly into painting, but he'd play the guitar sometimes and I got him to teach me in exchange for studio work."

"Like what?"

"Cleaning brushes, stretching canvases. Tidying up after him – he was the messiest artist in the whole place!"

"Are you tidy?"

Sam grimaced. "No! But I learnt to be. Worth it, for the guitar lessons. He left after a couple of years though – 'in search of a new muse'. I always thought his playing was better than his painting, but

I couldn't exactly tell him that."

"So, are you going to be a musician then?"

Several expressions passed swiftly across Sam's face – eagerness, fake indifference, resignation. Avril sensed this meant a lot to him, even as he shrugged.

"I dunno."

She looked at the deskscreen. The tech looked old, but Avril could tell it was running a program for creating music tracks.

"You've been recording." She stated the obvious. "You're a composer and you're going to be a performer."

Sam stared at her, his eyes bright. "You say that like it's a fact. Like it's true."

"It's going to be." She shrugged. "You might as well admit it."

"Can you tell the future?" His voice was hushed, as if he thought she might be a witch.

"No!" she laughed. "I just mean, you obviously love music and you're obviously good at it. So it would be weird if you stopped doing it. If you didn't perform one day."

"Oh. I guess..." He half-smiled, as if to soften his next words. "You're a bit odd, you know?"

"Oh yes," Avril agreed. "Even my family say so. And I suspect they're all quite peculiar too."

For a moment there was silence. Avril swivelled the chair gently and looked at the multiple layers of audio waves hovering on the deskscreen.

"What's your ambition then?" said Sam, suddenly.

She grinned broadly. "That would be telling."

"Oh come on! I've told you mine!" he said. "I'm going to be – no, I am – a musician! There, I've said it."

He glowed with energy, and Avril met his excitement with her own confession. "I want to travel!"

"Where?"

"Everywhere!" She swept her arm in a grand gesture, encompassing the whole world. "I've barely even been out of Home Valley. Town is the furthest I've been, and there are whole other countries – continents – to explore!"

"Home Valley?" Sam picked up on the phrase.

Avril ignored him, hurrying to cover her mistake.

"I want to travel by dirigible and train and boat, all over the world. I want to hear other languages and meet people who live completely differently to how we do. I want to go where the wind takes me, and never be tied down by the planting rotation or chores schedule or harvest time ever again!"

"That sounds–"

BANG BANG BANG!

Sam was interrupted by aggressive hammering on the front door below. They looked at each other.

"Who's that?" asked Avril.

"I don't know." Sam sounded fearful. "Not my family."

He moved his guitar and knelt on the bed to look

out of the window. Avril knelt beside him.

Two black-helmeted security guards were standing on the porch.

BANG BANG BANG!

One was using his truncheon to batter at the front door.

"Hey!" Sam called down. "What do you want?"

Avril touched his arm and pointed to the family Square.

"Sam. Look."

A massive lone AgriCarrier was standing by the little row of seedlings. They watched as its metal arm extended towards the ground.

"No!" shouted Sam.

"Come to the door." The security guard spoke in a loud monotone.

Sam hurtled down the stairs, Avril close behind. She could hear the whine of machinery and the scrape of steel on stone. Sam flung open the door and they ran down the steps, darting past the two guards standing at the top. At the edge of the Square, Sam and Avril stopped running and watched helplessly.

The metal scoop dragged along the ground, taking an entire layer with it: Avril's seedlings and soil were crushed into the huge bucket, the earth scraped bare as if the plants had never been there.

"What are you doing! You have no right–"

The guards descended, their boots heavy on the porch steps.

"Here." One of them held out a sheaf of paper.

Sam ignored it so Avril took it.

"What are you doing!" Sam yelled again.

"You have unauthorised soil and crops on your land. The terms of your contract with GreenCult state that these are not permitted and have therefore been removed."

"What contract?"

"All the information is in the document."

Avril scanned some of the pages, trying to make sense of it.

...now, therefore, in consideration of the mutual covenants and promises herein contained, and other good and valuable consideration, the receipt and sufficiency of which are hereby acknowledged, the parties hereto agree as follows...

"Stop!" Sam shouted. "Stop! Stop!"

The vehicle had tipped the poor mashed plants into its open back and was turning around on the family Square, its massive caterpillar tracks compacting the earth and leaving deep zigzags in the ground. The guards marched towards it and hopped up onto their perches, clinging to the side of the AgriCarrier as it picked up speed.

"Come back!" Sam's voice was ragged and desperate.

He ran down the road after them, the truck easily pulling away, the guards impassive. After a few hundred metres, he stopped and stood completely still, staring after the disappearing vehicle, his hands hanging useless.

Avril looked at the dejected hunch of his shoulders and felt her heart twist in her chest. For a moment she was sad enough to start sobbing right there in the road, then fury overwhelmed her so quickly she felt breathless. She ran to Sam and grabbed his shoulder.

"Come with me."

FIVE

Sam

Sam had never felt so angry or so helpless in his life. He grabbed the papers from Avril and looked blindly at them, eyes sliding off the incomprehensible legal jargon.

"It doesn't make sense," said Avril. "It's nonsense, business speak."

Sam scrunched the sheaf in his hand and made an incoherent sound of rage.

"Come on," said Avril. "Grab your bike. I want to show you something."

Her green eyes were dark with urgency and her mouth was set in a determined line. Sam couldn't guess what she was thinking. He had a feeling that if he didn't go with her now, she might never offer again.

"Okay," he decided. "I need to leave a message for my parents first."

He ran up the steps, leaving the door open. Avril watched him flatten the crumpled papers on the small hall table and scribble something on the front page. He took a key from a hook on the wall and secured the front door behind him.

"Where are we going?" he said, jumping the four steps in one leap.

"You lock your doors?"

"You don't?"

Avril retrieved her bike from the road and waited while Sam fetched his from behind the house. As soon as he reappeared, she pushed off and began cycling fast towards the waterhole. Sam caught her up quickly and they settled into the same urgent pace. Sam looked sideways at her, wanting to break the silence but conscious that she always shied away from questions. He tried to think of a simple one that she couldn't dodge.

"Are we going to your home?"

"Yes," she said, clamping her mouth shut as if uttering the single word had taken all her energy.

Sam had the feeling he shouldn't question further. They pedalled on for over half an hour until the waterhole came into view. Sam's top was sticking to his back and he felt hot and grimy with desert dust. The pool was blue and clear, and the tumbling noise of the waterfall sounded like an invitation.

"You want to swim?" he asked.

Avril shook her head. She pulled up alongside a group of large bushes and dismounted, then hid her bike behind the foliage.

"Should I put mine there too?"

"Yeah – no, wait. Hang on." Avril took off her hat and ran a hand over her hair, smoothing it down then replacing the cap.

He waited, watching as the determination on her face wavered into anxiety; she was playing for time.

"What's up?" he asked.

For an answer, she turned her back on him and went to sit cross-legged on a rock by the water.

"Avril!"

He dumped his bike on the ground and followed, sitting next to her on the warm stone. "What's going on?"

Avril looked at him, her eyes anguished.

"Can I trust you?" she said.

"What? Yes! Of course!"

"No, but seriously. Truly seriously. I hardly know you–"

Without thinking, Sam grabbed her hand. They stared at each other. Her hand was warm, the long slender fingers rough from farm work and carpentry. He was conscious of the guitar callouses on his own fingers, skin dry from weeding. Slowly, their fingers intertwined and Sam felt the breath catch in his throat. He swallowed.

"You can trust me. I promise."

Avril leaned towards him a little.

"The place I'm going to take you is so secret that if anyone discovers I've told you, I'll be in the worst trouble you can imagine!"

"I'll never tell anyone. I promise."

Sam squeezed her hand and felt her gently return the pressure.

"But you don't have to take risks for me. I'll understand if you can't–"

"I want to. Because – because you need to understand," she said. "Come on. Hide your bike. Let's go."

Sam didn't want to let go of her hand, but they both released their grip and jumped off the rock. While Sam stashed his bike behind the bushes, Avril started climbing up the cliff from the water's edge.

"Follow me!" she called, giving a wave.

She didn't even need to use her hands, the rock face seemed so familiar to her. Sam scrambled over the rocks, and soon they were both balanced near the waterfall.

"Here."

Sam watched, amazed, as Avril slid behind the water and disappeared. He took a step sideways, placing his feet exactly where she'd just been standing, and peered to see where she'd gone. There, behind the curtain of water, was a ledge and, standing on it, a shadow-Avril waited, obscured by a film of spray.

Sam felt less than confident.

"Come on!"

Avril's voice was muffled by the boom of water.

He psyched himself up, and just then a pale arm stretched out along the cliff face towards him. He took her hand and stepped behind the waterfall.

"Oh!"

The cold water was a shock. It caught the side of his body, drenching his left arm and leg and half his back. Avril laughed and let go of his hand. She was completely dry.

"Don't worry," she said. "It's a knack."

Sam shook his head and laughed too. He looked around. The water flew down in front of them, a perpetual torrent. Behind Avril, a narrow opening yawned into the rock.

"This way."

Sam followed her into the tunnel, keeping his hand on the craggy wall and feeling a prickle of fear as they moved away from the watery light. He was relieved when Avril snapped a torch on, even more so when the tunnel widened and they could walk next to each other. The air was chill after the warmth of the sun and Sam's wet left side was freezing from the waterfall soaking. It was midnight-dark. Avril navigated the forks and twists of the journey without hesitation, and Sam kept close beside her.

"So... Uh... Do you live in these caves?"

Avril's laugh echoed and bounced around the cavernous space.

"No! Don't be ridiculous!"

"But – but they are the secret? Aren't they?"

She stopped and looked at him, the torchlight making her straw hair glow and her eyes glitter.

"They're part of the secret. You must never show anyone the way. None of the Townids has ever found–"

"Townids?"

It was hard to tell in the gloom, but Sam was pretty sure Avril blushed.

"Sorry – that's what we call Town Kids."

"We?"

"Me and my siblings and cousins. The whole family does, to be honest." She wrinkled her nose. "Do you mind?"

Sam shrugged and shook his head. "Can you tell me about your family?"

Avril started walking again. "Come on, let's keep going."

For a moment, Sam thought she was going to ignore the question completely, as usual. But she sighed and added, "I'll tell you as we walk."

He kept pace with her, treading carefully on the uneven, rocky floor. It felt like she was never going to speak, but he resisted the urge to press her and after a few minutes she started talking.

"These tunnels lead to Home Valley, the farm

where me and my family live. We're cut off from Newbeck town by Cragg Hills, and that's how my parents want it. There's a road out on the other side of the valley, but it's closed off."

"Why?"

"When I was younger, we were raided."

Sam couldn't see her expression, but her voice sounded tight.

"What do you mean?"

"Strangers came at night and attacked us. They stole all our crops, destroyed everything, years of work."

"Sounds scary."

"It was! We had nothing left. That winter, we had to rely on rations. We were so hungry. My dad swore it would never happen again, so he hid the way into the valley, blocked the road. Since then, we've kept everything secret."

"How many of you are there?"

"Me, two brothers, one sister. Natasha, Dustin and Ben. And there's my grandparents, plus Ma's sister, Jodi, and her husband, Frank. After the raid, Fa's brother, David, and his wife Nessa moved to the valley to help rebuild. So that's another household."

"So, your family, plus your grandparents, plus two aunts and uncles. Four households?"

"That's right. And six cousins."

"Six!" Sam adjusted his mental picture of Avril's isolation.

"Yep. All living in Home Valley."

"So are all the kids home-schooled like you?"

"Yeah. Well, they were. They're all older than me, apart from my little cousins, Lexie and Christo. They're too small for schooling. My other cousins and siblings have finished education, not that they all wanted to."

"How come?"

"Natasha started university but she was brought home when the raid happened. Dustin wanted to go to college and Ben's desperate to train in mechanics, but Fa won't let them."

"Your Fa sounds tough."

"Yep. And narrow-minded. He wants everyone to stay in the valley and farm it forever. Every time he plants a tree, he calls it a 'legacy', as if he thinks we'll all still be here in fifty years' time looking after it."

"Fifty years!"

"Exactly! And I..." She trailed off.

"You–?"

"I just want to get out of there!"

Her impassioned words reverberated along the tunnel they were passing through. Sam didn't know what to say.

"I'm beyond suffocated," Avril said, after a moment.

A line of light glowed ahead. A fork in the tunnel. The glow intensified as they approached, and Avril flicked off the torch.

They were nearly at the turning in the tunnel and Sam slowed his pace. Suddenly, he felt hesitant. He didn't want to get Avril in trouble with her family, though he was curious to see how they managed their Squares.

"I know how you feel," said Sam. "I mean, it isn't the same, but my family don't get my music at all."

"Really?"

Avril matched her footsteps to his and they ambled towards the bright opening.

"Yeah. They call it a 'fun hobby'."

She grimaced. "Ouch."

"Exactly! They pretend to listen when I play them compositions, but I can tell they don't understand. My mum even said Are you sure you don't want a basketball hoop when I asked for a guitar pedal for my birthday!"

"And you don't even like basketball!"

"Right!"

Avril snorted, which made Sam laugh too.

"But because my brother Casey does, and my mates at school, and – well, basically almost everyone else my age in Newbeck..."

"...You must like it too?"

"Yeah. According to impressive parental logic."

"Just like I must love farming, because every single other person in my family was born with a trowel in their hand!"

They stood still at the bend in the tunnel, looking

at each other. Sam liked how Avril's eyes laughed with shared understanding and found himself smiling at her. She reached out and took his hand, and his skin tingled.

"We're here," she said.

"Are you sure you want to do this?" said Sam. "It's not too late for me to go back."

"I'm sure. We'll keep out of sight. No-one will know I've brought you."

Without hesitating, she pulled him around the corner into the final short stretch. Bright sunlight poured through the mouth of the tunnel, dazzling him. As they approached the opening, Sam's eyes adjusted. The rock framed a stunning view of blue sky and green land, greener than anything he'd ever seen. Not only that, the huge valley contained more shades of green than he'd even known existed.

There were no Squares.

Trees, dense with new leaves, were dotted everywhere, and in some places even clustered together in large groups. The land undulated like a runkled blanket over pillows, falling into uneven areas, each planted with different greens. Pale green and dark green, thick shiny green and wispy feathery green, hedges and grass and crops and plants that Sam didn't recognise. There were even pinks and purples in the ground near the weather-beaten buildings on the far side of the valley. One of the buildings, made entirely of glass, winked in the sunshine.

"Uh..." Sam tried to say something, but his mouth just dropped open and nothing comprehensible emerged.

It was as if he'd never been in true daylight before, as if he'd lived all his life behind a gauze and suddenly the curtain was drawn back, revealing how colours should look. It was the most beautiful thing he'd ever seen.

Avril looked at him, biting her lip. "What do you think?"

"Uh?"

"I wanted to show you... the difference?"

She sounded so uncertain that Sam's amazement fell away, and he laughed. "It's definitely different!"

Avril looked relieved. "Come on, let's go somewhere we can't be seen."

They ran across scrubby grass to a neat fence, on the other side of which stood a vast tree, its arms spreading bigger than a house. The ancient trunk was fat and twisted, with low branches that made it easy for them to climb up and sit among the leaves.

Avril rummaged in her pocket and pulled out a small tub. "Here." She offered it to Sam.

He peered at the contents. "What are they?"

"Dried apple rings. Aren't you hungry?"

"Yes." Sam took one quickly. He couldn't imagine not being hungry. The white circle was chewy and sweet. He regretted eating it so fast.

"Have the rest."

Avril put one in her mouth and gave him the pot.

"Are you sure?" Sam was incredulous.

"We have loads more in the larder."

Sam ate another, slowly savouring the flavour, and tried to imagine what it must be like to have unlimited food. He'd had apples occasionally, when they were included in fresh rations, but he'd never seen them growing. He had a feeling they grew on trees.

"Is this an apple tree?"

"No." She looked at him curiously. "It's an oak. It's hundreds of years old. Those are apple trees, that cluster over there."

"I can see why you weren't very impressed with the trees on Main Street."

He looked at the fertile land stretching away from them. In the distance, a small group of black spidery objects whirred in the air.

"What are they?"

"Drones," said Avril. "My brother, Dustin, uses aerial imaging to monitor crop health and productivity."

Sam whistled. "Impressive."

Avril shrugged. "Standard issue. Like the ground-level monitoring network."

"The what?"

She pointed to one of the fields.

"See the spikes spaced along the furrows, there? The antennae transmit information from the sensors – stuff like water levels and soil temperature. My favourite gadgets are the LaserWeeders. You know how little robots are almost like pets?"

Sam really didn't, but Avril chattered on.

"Well, I've given them all names. Prospero, Pericles, Aerial and Puck. Farm tech is the only thing my family ever spends money on."

Sam's mind reeled. Not only was the valley completely different from the beige flatness of Newbeck, but it also seemed to be operating with an almost futuristic level of technology.

"Did you say your parents own this place?"

"My grandparents bought the land when the Government first introduced the Squares scheme. They got it cheap, because it was classed as infertile. The soil quality was poor, and the area is hilly and hard to farm."

"This is poor quality soil?"

"Not anymore. Family legend tells how they transformed it with hard work blah blah blah."

Avril sounded dismissive, as if what she'd said was a boring old story rather than a total revelation.

"WHAT?"

She looked perplexed. "My parents always go on about–"

"You can transform soil? What do you mean?"

"Of course you can! With compost, manure, mulching, crop rotation, cover crops–"

It was like she was discussing an unfamiliar sport with rules he'd never heard of. Sam was about to stop her, to ask what on earth she meant, when a deep voice cut them off with a ferocious bellow.

"WHO THE HELL ARE YOU?!"

Avril's pale face went a blotchy red.

"Fa!"

"GET DOWN HERE RIGHT NOW!"

Beneath the oak tree, staring up at them, stood a man with no hair and the build of a boxer, holding a thick wooden staff. Hurrying up the field was a woman with a ponytail the same colour as Avril's.

"It's my parents," said Avril in a horror-filled voice. "Come on, we have to get down."

Sam felt a pang of terror as he followed Avril and scrambled to the ground.

"Josh, what's going on?" said Avril's mum.

"I don't know, Sophie," said Avril's dad, sounding menacing. "Our daughter is about to tell us."

Avril and Sam stood in front of the tree. Sam wished he had the confidence to grab her hand but couldn't stop looking at the ridged scar on her dad's bald skull. Her dad slapped his staff against his palm in a threatening way as he surveyed them.

"I can explain–" Sam started, desperate to protect Avril.

"Shut up!" said Josh. Thwack went the stick. "I want to hear from my daughter."

"Fa, this is Sam. I..." Avril's voice was as trembly as the oak leaves. She trailed off.

"A Townid?"

Avril nodded.

"What were you thinking? How could you? How could you bring him here? Now they'll all come!"

Avril's dad paced in front of them, muscular and intimidating as a lion.

"No! No, they won't!" Avril's voice returned. "You have to understand! GreenCult, they stole Sam's soil, the seedlings I gave him–"

"You've been giving away our plants?" Josh was shouting now. "Taking our crops and giving them to a Townid?"

"It was only six tiny plants! I wanted to help! They need our help – GreenCult is–"

"They have only themselves to blame!" bellowed Josh. "It is not our job to help those urban idiots!"

"Why not?" Avril yelled back. "Why are you so selfish?"

Avril's mum raised her hands in a peacekeeping gesture. "Avril! Josh! Calm down, both of you. Stop shouting!"

"Don't you understand?" Josh stood still, dropping his voice to a low rumble and eyeballing Avril. "You've put us all in danger. They'll all want what we have. They'll all come–"

"Er, no," Sam interjected. "I can't bring anyone here. I don't know the way."

Josh looked at him as if he were insane.

"You're here, aren't you?"

"Yes, but I couldn't navigate those caves on my

own. It's a labyrinth in there. Not sure how I'm going to get home, to be honest."

Avril gave Sam a grateful look. There was silence.

Josh gave a decisive thump on the ground with his staff. "This is what's going to happen." His fierce eyes dared anyone to disagree. "I will take you back to the waterhole, Townid boy–"

"Sam!" said Avril.

"Townid boy!" Josh continued. "Blindfolded."

Sam swallowed.

"You will never come here again. You will never enter the caves. You will never attempt to find your way through them. You will never tell anyone what you have seen. Understood?"

Sam nodded.

Josh turned on Avril. "You are forbidden to enter the caves until further notice."

"Fa–"

"AND you are confined to the farmhouse for the next week."

"But–"

"NO ARGUMENTS."

Avril closed her mouth, and Sam saw a tear caught in her lower eyelashes. He felt terrible.

"Sophie, please fetch something from the farmhouse that we can use as a blindfold," said Josh.

"There's some cloth in the Upper Fields shed," said Avril, quickly. "I'll go. I know where it is."

"Be quick."

Avril sprinted away.

"You're being very tough on them, Josh," said Sophie.

"With good reason! Or do you think Avril's behaviour is acceptable?"

"No, of course not," she said. "But stop yelling. It makes you sound Neanderthal."

A painful silence followed. Sam could feel sweat making its way slowly down the path of his spine. He tried once more to stand up for Avril.

"It wasn't Avril's fault," he said. "She–"

"Yes," Josh cut him off. "It was."

The next few minutes were excruciating.

Gradually, in the quiet, Sam realised that although no-one was speaking, the air was full of sounds. Birds were singing all over the valley. Crickets chirped. The leaves of the oak tree rustled and whispered in the breeze. It was extraordinary. Despite his fear, Sam drank in the birdsong, trying to memorise the trills. Then he heard running feet and strained breathing – it was Avril, sprinting towards them, pink-cheeked and out of breath.

She came up beside him and lifted the stiff beige fabric, about to tie it around his head.

"I'll do that," said Josh.

"No, let me," Sophie interrupted.

Quickly, Avril stepped in front of Sam, saying, "Here."

As she passed the fabric across to her mother,

Avril used her body to hide another movement, secretly shoving something into Sam's hand before she stepped away. He closed his fingers around the folded paper, and looked at her, trying to convey how sorry he was and how glad he was to know her and how he didn't want to say goodbye, all through a single helpless gaze. Avril's eyes were the last thing he saw before the rough canvas obscured his sight.

The journey through the caves felt a hundred times longer than before. The floor was rougher and more uneven than ever, and Avril's dad didn't seem to care if Sam tripped or scraped himself on jutting rock walls. Sam had managed to stash Avril's paper in his pocket, and stumbled along with both hands outstretched, Josh's iron grip bruising his upper arm. The man didn't say a word, and all Sam could hear was the tread and scuffle of their feet on the stone.

When the sound of splashing water reached his ears, Sam was filled with relief. Eventually he could feel damp spray on his hands and then Josh was untying the scratchy material. They were standing on the ledge.

"Never come back."

Sam nodded, hating him.

Avril's dad watched him climb out from behind the water and make his way down to the water-hole. Sam didn't want to reveal the hiding place for Avril's bike, so he pretended to be walking to town and trudged a few hundred metres along the track before looking round to see that Josh had gone. He doubled back to get his cycle from the bushes and, before setting off home, sat on the rock by the water and unfolded the little scrap of paper.

It was torn from a brown envelope and on one side was printed in black ink:

Carrot seeds – Chantenay.

On the other side, scrawled in pencil, was a single sentence:

Meet me at the waterhole at dawn.

SIX

Avril

The familiar blackness of the caves felt welcoming after the creepy dark of the fields outside. Avril knew the farm better than anything in the world, but in the pre-dawn nighttime it had felt alien and hostile. Sneaking out of the farmhouse had been terrifying, every floor creak sounding loud as a shout. The greenhouse door screeched and the gates she'd climbed over had all complained. But Avril had reached the old oak tree without waking anyone, and the torchlit tunnels were a safe haven after crossing gardens and fields in full view of the buildings.

Her rucksack was heavy, dragging at her shoulders, but she kept a quick pace, hurrying towards the waterfall, trying not to acknowledge the fear lurking at the edge of her mind.

What if he didn't come?

He liked her. He'd promised she could trust him, and he'd tried to stand up for her when they were caught. Surely he would come? But she'd walked him into terrible trouble. He'd been yelled at and accused and called an idiot Townid. It must've been horrible, being dragged blindfolded through the tunnels by Fa. Maybe Sam was furious with her. Maybe he wouldn't come.

And what would she do then?

She pushed the thought away. The sound of water bounced towards her, and she realised there was a faint glow of light in the tunnel ahead. The sun had risen while she was inside the hills. She walked even faster.

He was sitting on the flat rock by the water's edge, looking away from her towards the dim hulk of Newbeck town on the horizon. The sun wasn't visible over Cragg Hills yet, but a grey glimmer lightened the sky. Perhaps further east, sunbeams were already touching the fields in the valley.

Avril wanted to call out to Sam, but the early morning air felt cool and secretive – irrationally, she was scared her family might hear if she shouted. So, she climbed swiftly down the rocks and, by the time she reached the bottom, he'd heard her approach and was up on his feet. They met on the rock and stood facing each other, somehow holding hands – although Avril wasn't sure who had reached out first, how her hands had met his.

"Hi," she said, and found she was whispering.

"Hi," he whispered back.

Birds sang in the pause between them.

"Have you been waiting long?"

"A little while. Wasn't sure what time dawn was. Didn't want to miss you."

"Thanks for coming." She looked away. "I'm so sorry about my father, about–"

"Hey, stop it. It's fine. It wasn't your fault."

"I feel terrible!"

"Well, don't! I'm glad we went. I'm glad I saw it."

"Really?"

"Of course!"

Avril met his gaze and found herself holding her breath. Then she was leaning towards him in the exact same way that he was leaning towards her, and their noses bumped and their lips met and for a moment they stood, pressed together in a kiss. Avril held her breath and, when they broke apart, felt herself shiver with a sensation more hot than cold.

She wondered what Sam was thinking, whether he felt the same inner tingle. When he spoke, his voice sounded as tentative as she felt.

"D'you want to sit down?"

"Sure."

Avril took the heavy bag off her back and lowered it to the ground. They sat on the rock, Sam's shoulder warm against hers.

"It's beautiful, your valley," he said.

She sighed. "Yeah, I know. Just – it felt like a beautiful prison. Sometimes."

"Felt? Past tense?"

Avril scrunched up her face. "Um, yeah. Kind of?"

Sam looked at the rucksack. "You're running away. Right?"

She nodded, lacing her fingers around her knees. "You heard him, a whole week indoors – I couldn't! I'd die!"

"And not seeing me. That'd be enough to kill anyone."

She laughed. "Well, actually, I'm nearly dead after those hours away from you."

"I'm not surprised. I am, basically, oxygen."

"Right."

"Right."

Then they were kissing again and Avril was held in a feeling of rightness, given certainty by the warm pressure of Sam's lips. When she opened her eyes, the dawn halo edging the top of Cragg Hills had begun to glow gold. Day was approaching. Soon her parents would get up and discover her empty bed. What would they do? What was she going to do? She shivered.

"Come to my house," said Sam.

Avril was washed with relief. "Can I? Are you sure?"

"You have to."

He stood and held out his hand, pulling her to her feet, then picked up her rucksack.

"Woah! What have you got in here? Rocks?"

Avril took the bulging bag from him. "No! Books. And clothes, and maps, and a few tools... Quite a lot of things, actually. I didn't know what I'd need. And something for you."

She opened the flap and unwrapped the corner of a large fabric bundle sitting snugly at the top of the rucksack.

"Seedlings," said Sam.

His smile caused a skin-spark just between her shoulder blades.

"You're running away from home in the middle of the night and you stopped to bring plants? You're mad!"

"I'm SO angry with GreenCult for smashing the other ones. I thought maybe we could find somewhere secret to plant these? I brought more this time."

"You're mad!" he said again. "And probably hungry?"

"Starving! I was going to pack some food, but my parents' bedroom is right over the kitchen and all the cupboard doors squeak."

"Let's go to mine. We can have breakfast before my family wake up, then you can hide in my room while we figure out…"

"Everything?"

"Yeah."

Sam's bike was lying by the rock. Avril retrieved her refurbished-wreck from behind the bushes and returned to find him wearing the rucksack on his back.

"It's my bag. I can carry it."

"But you already carried it all the way here, through the valley and tunnels, and it weighs a ton."

"Because I packed too much. It's my fault it's heavy, so I should carry it."

"But you packed seedlings for me, so I should carry it."

"Fine." She gave in with a smile.

They set off towards town. The sun was peeping over the top of the hills, warming their backs as they cycled side by side.

Sam eased the key into the lock and gently opened the front door. He beckoned Avril to follow him into the hallway and closed the door behind them with silent stealth. Tiptoeing, they turned off the hall into the kitchen and froze.

"Well!"

"Well!"

Sam's parents exclaimed their surprise in unison. Avril remembered their names: Dexter and Lily. They were seated at the kitchen table, poring over piles of papers.

"What are you doing up so early?" blurted Sam.

"I might ask the same of you!" said Sam's dad.

"You've been out? At this time?" Sam's mum sounded anxious. "Where have you been? And what's Avril doing visiting at such an hour? Is something wrong?"

Sam was silent. Avril, standing behind him in the doorway, had no idea what to say.

"Not that you're not welcome–" Lily added kindly, only to be interrupted by Dexter.

"But it isn't exactly the usual time to be seeing friends! Sam, what's going on?"

"I'll put the kettle on," said Lily, sounding like she was reaching for normality. "Sit down, both of you."

Sam cast a look at Avril and let the rucksack slide to the floor. He took her hand, the expression on his face daring his parents to comment, and brought her to the kitchen table. They sat.

"What are the papers?" Sam asked.

"Never mind the–"

"The GreenCult contract–"

Dexter and Lily both answered at the same time then stopped. The kettle started to chunter.

"It's because of GreenCult," said Sam. "That's why Avril's here."

"Go on," said Dexter, listening intently.

"You know how they stole the seedlings yesterday?"

"Uh huh." Dexter nodded.

"Well, me and Avril were – we were really angry. So, Avril took me to see–" He stopped.

Avril could tell that Sam didn't want to break his promise to her dad.

"I showed Sam a different way of farming. My family don't have Squares."

"Ah." Dexter exhaled, as if things were starting to make sense. "Which is why you have such good soil."

"And different crops." Lily sat down.

The kettle reached its bubbling crescendo. Dexter stood up and poured boiling water into the teapot, bringing it to the table with mugs. They all sat and exchanged awkward glances.

"So where is–"

Sam cut off his mum's question. "We can't say. We promised not to tell."

"I brought some more seedlings," Avril chipped in, by way of an apology. "But I guess they'll need to be planted somewhere secret."

"Ah! No!" Lily sounded triumphant. "No, they won't!"

"But what about GreenCult?" asked Sam.

"We've been going through the contracts," said Lily.

"Your mother couldn't sleep after what happened yesterday," said Dexter, sounding rueful. "Dragged me out of bed to go through the paperwork. As if I know one end of a contract from another!"

"I've read every word of every contract from the past five years," said Lily, gesturing to the papers spread out all over the tabletop. "Not one of them actually prohibits the use of alternative soil sources or non-selected crops."

"Then why did they bulldoze our Square?" said Sam, furious.

"Bullying tactics," said Dexter. "Hoping we'll be too scared to protest."

"Exactly," said Lily. "They're relying on the fact that no-one ever reads the small print. That their contracts are such gobbledegook it's almost impossible to make sense of them. But I've checked the national legal precedents too – it's illegal to have the kind of monopoly they're claiming. So even if the contract did say we have to use their seeds and their seeds only, it wouldn't stand up in court."

"So they were the ones breaking the law?" said Avril.

"That's right," said Lily, nodding furiously.

"Though I don't see how we'd get to tell them that, what with all the machinery and security guards..." Dexter pointed out.

There was a brief, considering pause.

"Anyway!" Dexter interrupted his own silence and gave Sam and Avril a fierce stare. "What were you two doing out and about in the middle of the night?"

Sam looked warily at Avril, and she decided on a pared-down version of the truth.

"We met at dawn—"

"Early morning, not the middle of the night—" Sam backed her up.

"So I could bring these replacement seedlings." Avril stood and went over to her rucksack. "Because later in the day I'll be busy. You know how it gets in springtime…"

She lifted out the large fabric bundle and brought it to the table.

"Can we see?" Lily said.

"It's a bit muddy."

"Never mind. Show us!"

Lily moved the mugs to the side and Dexter started pouring tea from the pot while Avril placed the parcel in the middle of the tabletop. She unfolded the cloth, then carefully lifted the protective straw inside, revealing the plants nestled within. There were different sizes and species, all with soil clinging to their roots and a few small leaves at the top of each stem.

"So many!" said Lily, her voice hushed.

"Twenty-ish," said Avril. "Not that many, really.

Just four of each. Strawberries and tomatoes, to re-place the other ones. And courgettes, runner beans, and squash. Oh, and this–"

She rummaged in the straw and pulled out what looked like a long dead twig with hairy sprouts at one end.

"A raspberry cane. Won't fruit this year, but it's perennial. It'll spread and come back, so next year you'll have a whole berry patch."

Lily clasped Dexter's hand. His forehead furrowed and he spoke slowly.

"I'm not sure we can accept. I mean, your parents must want these."

"They don't mind at all!" Avril lied. "We have so many, honestly. The greenhouse is bursting with seedlings!" She managed a fake laugh. "We throw away the small ones when we thin them out, so these would just be going to waste. You're doing us a favour, really."

She picked up the mug of green tea that had been placed in front of her and buried her nose in it, try-ing to avoid eye contact. Dexter continued to look suspicious.

"It's fine, Dad," said Sam. "I met Avril's parents yesterday and they're – really nice."

"Oh Dexter," said Lily, "just look at these beau-tiful plants. This would be life changing. Surely it can't do any harm." She turned to Avril. "I mean, if you're sure–"

"Oh yes!"

"Hmm." Dexter made a low growling sound that Avril couldn't interpret, but which Lily and Sam seemed to know as acquiescence. Lily gave a laugh of delight and stood up.

"I don't know about you kids, but I'm starving! Who's for breakfast?"

"Great," said Sam. "Avril?"

"Yes, please." At the thought of food, her stomach at once remembered how hungry it was and she pressed her hand against it to stop it rumbling.

"Dexter, can you wake Casey? He needs to eat before school."

Dexter went upstairs, and Avril watched as Sam helped his mum get ingredients from the cupboards, curious to see what they were making. Yellow liquid was poured from the tap of a small barrel labelled Bacterial Culture, then combined with water and a grey substance like heavy flour, all heated in a pan on the electric hob.

When Sam began pouring the beige slop into bowls, Avril almost thought it was a joke. When the family took up spoons and began eating, even smiling as they did so, she decided it must taste a thousand times better than it looked.

It didn't.

"You okay?" said Sam, scooping another dollop into his mouth.

Avril was trying not to gag. "Mm-huh." She

nodded, managing to swallow.

Sam's brother, Casey, had just appeared looking grumpy, his cheek crumpled with pillow-marks, but was now eating the fastest of all of them.

"Vitamins?" he said, between mouthfuls.

"Here." Sam passed a large jar across the table.

Casey put an orange pill in his mouth; Avril watched as the pot was passed around, every family member taking their dose.

"D'you want one?" said Sam.

It seemed to be expected, so Avril took one. "Thanks."

The flavour was strong and artificial, the texture almost fizzy on her tongue. Weirdest of all, it was familiar. Where had she tasted it before?

"Have you had enough porridge?" asked Sam's mum.

That's not porridge! thought Avril.

"Oh, er, yes," Avril said, looking at the other empty bowls. "Sorry, I'm not as hungry as I thought."

"I'll have it!" said Casey, quickly starting to eat the rest of her portion. "Sportsmen need extra protein."

"Sportsmen!" Sam mocked.

"Protein?" said Avril.

"Bacterial Culture," said Lily. "Don't you use it at home?"

"Er, I'm not sure."

"It's the best protein source," said Casey with his

mouth full. "Apart from meat."

"Don't start! I don't care if you do want to be a professional basketball player," Dexter interrupted. "The ban on industrial animal farming is still the best thing the government's ever done!"

"True," Lily agreed. "It's been decades, and the river is only just recovering from the chicken factory pollution."

"I'm not saying I want megafarms back!" complained Casey, "I just–"

He was interrupted by a noise that made them all jump.

BANG BANG BANG!

Someone was pounding violently at the door.

"GreenCult?" said Sam, jumping up so quickly his chair fell over.

"Again?" said Avril. "Why?"

Then she froze. A familiar voice was shouting outside.

"I KNOW YOU HAVE MY DAUGHTER IN THERE! OPEN THE DOOR!"

It was Fa.

SEVEN

Sam

Avril looked terrified. Sam jumped to his feet. His family were staring at Avril as if her skin had suddenly sprouted leaves.

"It's okay, Avril," Sam said. "We won't let them in."

The hammering at the door repeated, then a female voice called, "Avril, darling! Please come out!"

"OPEN THIS DOOR!"

"Are those your parents?"

Sam could hear the nerves in his mum's voice.

"Uhhh..." Avril, twisting her hands in her lap, cast a desperate glance at Sam.

Feeling helpless, he tried to sound strong. "Yes. I think Avril's parents are outside."

Sam wasn't sure whether the minutes that followed were more painful for him or for Avril. Both sets of parents were furious.

Avril's mum and dad had found her bed empty and driven to town in the hope of tracking her down. The distinctive bike-disguised-as-a-wreck lying on the path outside had led them to Sam's house. When Avril's parents came into the kitchen, Josh's eyes bulged at the sight of the seedlings resting in straw on the table.

"I take it those are ours?"

"I'm so sorry," Sam's mum gasped.

At that moment, Sam hated Josh for hurting his mother.

"Avril told us you didn't mind," she said, "that these were going spare."

"Spare!" Josh snorted. "We don't have anything to–"

"But we DO! We DO have plants to spare!" Avril slammed her hand on the table. "How can you be so selfish? Everyone in Newbeck scrapes and struggles to raise just a few crops on their Squares. They aren't allowed to choose, they aren't allowed more than four types of plant, they aren't allowed perennials – they have to buy soil!"

"That's right," said Sam, standing beside her.

"The whole thing is evil and corrupt! GreenCult

is so scared of anyone discovering other ways to farm that they bully people if they even try! When I brought six tiny seedlings, and Sam planted them in a minuscule patch of proper soil, the corporation sent two guards and an AgriCarrier to dig them up! They smashed the plants to smithereens, stole the soil and took it away. And they pretended they had the right to do it – that it was in the contract!"

Avril came to a breathless halt.

Silence.

Josh and Sophie looked stunned.

After a moment, Sophie found her voice. "Is that true?"

"Oh yes." Sam's parents nodded. "That's exactly what happened."

There was another silence.

"Do you – do you really buy soil?" asked Josh.

"Of course," said Dad, a touch of confusion in his voice. "Everyone does. Don't you?"

"No!" said Sophie, at the same time as Josh said, "That's private!"

There was another silence.

"We need to go," said Josh.

Sam watched as Mum went to re-wrap the seedlings, feeling enraged and helpless.

Sophie stopped her. "Please, keep them. It's the least we can do after causing such disruption."

Mum hesitated, then said, "That's very kind of you. I hope you understand, we don't want to take your crops. We don't want anything from you – except–"

She stopped, flinching under Josh's hostile gaze. Sam didn't know what she was going to say, but he willed her to continue.

"Except–" She swallowed and focused on Avril's mum. "If you did have any knowledge to share, about other ways of gardening – of farming – we'd be very grateful to learn from you."

Avril was staring at the floor. Sam tried to get her attention. What if this was the last time they'd be able to see each other? What if her dad really did lock her up at home? Sam felt as if the oxygen in the room was thinning out.

"Sam." His mum turned to him. "Take Avril into the living room, check she hasn't left anything behind. Casey, go upstairs."

Avril lifted her head. Sam gave Mum a look of gratitude and hurried into the hallway, Avril close behind him. They went into the next room and closed the door, adult voices rumbling through the wooden wall. Avril stood in the middle of the floor. The sorrowful look on her face made Sam's heart twist in his chest. He went to her and took her hands.

"Are you okay?"

She shrugged, but he felt her thumb lightly stroke his forefinger and a flicker of electric energy ran between them. They leaned closer and kissed, lips pressing softly together for just a moment.

Avril glanced at the door. "Your mum knows I didn't leave anything in here."

"Yeah. She's either giving us space, or she wants us out the way so she can talk privately to your folks."

Avril kissed him for longer this time, and Sam's spine tingled. They laced their fingers together and looked at each other. Sam was about to kiss her again when Avril broke away and paced the room in agitation.

"I can't bear it!"

"What?"

She suddenly felt so far away that Sam was worried he'd done something wrong.

"I'm going to have to go with them!"

He didn't know what to say.

"And they might never let me come to town again. What if I never see you again?"

She stopped pacing, looking utterly downcast. Sam crossed the room and put his arms around her, holding her tight. His heart was beating hard, loud enough that he thought she must be able to hear it. He wished he knew what to do. He released her and pulled his comscreen from his pocket.

"Give me your tag," he said.

"I don't have one," Avril wailed. "We use a closed comms system – everyone I know lives in Home Valley!"

"Can you get on the internet?"

"Yes. I have a deskscreen. For home ed stuff.

Studying."

"Then that's fine. We'll message."

Sam grabbed a piece of paper from the bureau and wrote his links on it.

"There."

Avril read what he'd written, holding the paper carefully, as if it might disintegrate in her hands.

"Alright," she said, folding the paper and tucking it into her trouser pocket.

"Message me any time. Day or night! Whenever you can. Just don't disappear again."

"What do you mean, again?" She clasped his hand, running her thumb over his knuckles once more, her eyes so serious he couldn't help smiling.

"The first couple of times we met, you appeared out of nowhere. Like, like–"

"Like an apparition? That's what you called me."

Sam felt a glow that she remembered their conversations.

"Exactly! And then you'd sort of evaporate again! Until you showed me the tunnels, it made no sense. I couldn't figure out where you were coming from."

"I won't disappear." She leaned forward and their lips touched.

There was a knock at the door.

"Time to go," said Sam's mum, without entering.

"Coming," Sam called back.

He looked at Avril. Without a word, they wrapped their arms around each other, pressing their bodies tightly together as they kissed again. Sam wished they never had to let go, but another knock at the door made them jump apart. Her face pale and set, Avril marched over and pulled it open. All the parents were standing in the hallway, Sophie holding Avril's rucksack. Without speaking, Avril took it from her and slung it on her back. Sam had never seen her eyes such a dark green.

The silence was worse than an out-of-tune instrument. Avril's mum looked uncomfortable, while her dad still seemed angry – though Sam was beginning to think perhaps Josh's face always wore that expression. He wondered what the adults had been talking about in their absence. He hoped they'd agreed that he and Avril could still see each other but it didn't seem likely. He scanned his parents' faces but couldn't tell what they were thinking.

Mum broke the silence. "Well, it was good to meet you."

"Likewise."

Sophie gave Mum a half-hug.

"Do think about it," Mum said to Avril's dad. "I hope we'll hear from you."

Josh didn't reply, but shook the hand she offered. Sam's dad raised his hand in farewell, putting his other palm on Sam's shoulder as if to console him. Sam's hopes plummeted. Whatever they'd talked about, the outcome wasn't good. He followed them all outside.

Josh picked up Avril's bike and put it in the back of an electric farm vehicle that was parked on the road in front of the house.

"We're driving?" said Avril.

"We came the long way round. Thought we'd need a vehicle," said her mum. "We didn't know how far you'd gone. And I can't imagine how you managed to get that bicycle through–"

She caught herself, glancing at Sam and his family.

"Come on."

Avril's dad gestured from the driving seat, demanding they hurry up. Avril gave Sam a final devastated look, walked to the vehicle and climbed in.

Sam broke away from his parents and ran to stand in the road, watching the trail of dust lengthen as Avril and her family drove away.

EIGHT

Avril

It was rare to have the whole family in one room at the same time. There weren't enough chairs. Today, Avril preferred to stand, anyway.

The journey home from Sam's had been horrible. Every time Avril had tried to speak, Fa had shut her down, saying, "We need to consult the family."

They had finished the drive in silence.

At one point, Ma had reached back from the front passenger seat to squeeze her knee, but Avril had no idea whether she was just being nice or whether she agreed that Fa was overreacting. As soon as they'd reached Home Valley, Fa had gone around the various farmhouses, banging on doors and summoning all her relations like an over-zealous medieval town crier.

Now, it felt like her stomach was a living origami as she waited for the Family Conference to begin. She leaned her back against the kitchen wall, arms crossed, and watched as Grandma and Grandpa fussed over Lexie and Christo, getting them to sit on laps. The aunts and uncles were all seated and Ma brought over the biggest tray, laden with mugs, and placed it in the centre of the table. Avril's three older siblings and the four grown-up cousins were bickering over who got the remaining chairs, until Uncle David intervened and made them all sit on stools.

Fa stood at the head of the table, waiting for everyone to settle. Eventually, he clapped his hands.

The family rustled into silence. Fa surveyed everyone, then made his announcement.

"I'm sorry to have to tell you all that Avril has put Home Valley in danger."

"WHAT?" Avril yelled over the gasps of shock that greeted his words. "That's not true! I only–"

Fa shouted her down. "You broke our rules, you went to town!"

Even more gasps and "Ohs" of surprise rippled around the table.

"More than once!"

He continued his attack. "And it wasn't on a whim. This was planned, premeditated! You must've been thinking about this for weeks. You refurbished a bike and somehow got it through the tunnels!"

Avril's brother Ben let out the annoying whistle he liked to give when he was impressed by someone else's wrongdoing.

"Worst of all–" Fa stopped looking at her and lowered his voice to address the family, as solemn as if she'd been worshipping Satan, "– she befriended a Townid family, stole plants from the greenhouse to give to them, and brought the son here."

"Oh, Avril!" Grandma's voice quivered with dismay.

"The greenhouse?" said Natasha, shocked.

"She showed him the way?" Grandpa was horrified.

"How could you?" said Aunt Jodi.

"You've put our home – this entire family – in danger!" boomed Fa. "We need to prepare to defend the valley."

"What?" Avril was staggered.

"Josh, I don't think–"

Fa interrupted Ma by slamming his fist on the table. "Don't you see? Those Townids won't keep a secret! Even if they don't come straight away, they'll bide their time."

"But Josh–"

"I'm telling you, at harvest time we can expect another raid!"

"Josh!" The sharp edge to Ma's voice prevented a third interruption. "Listen to me."

Fa clamped his mouth shut. Ma addressed everyone.

"We met a family in town, a mother and father and two boys. They were pleasant people."

Fa looked incredulous.

"I can't imagine any of them wanting to commit violent theft!" Ma said firmly.

"But if they tell other Townids…" said Aunt Jodi, sounding fearful as she trailed off.

Her husband, Frank, completed the thought. "… we could still be in danger. They might be nice, but their neighbours could be the ones who raided us!"

"Frank," Ma appealed to him. "We don't know that the raiders came from Newbeck. In fact, it's much more likely they were a gang from the city – remember the news reports! There was a lot of unrest that year, we weren't the only ones targeted."

"I still think Josh is right." Uncle Frank was obdurate. "We should be prepared."

Avril looked around the room at her family, their faces full of fear, confusion and anger, and her fingers tingled with the urge to become fists and fight.

"But they don't want our crops," she said, willing her relatives to understand. "They want our knowledge."

"Avril!" Fa tried to shut her up, but Ma spoke out.

"It's true," she agreed. "That's what the Townids we met wanted more than anything."

"What do you mean?" said Uncle David, speaking for the first time.

"GreenCult has a stranglehold on the business of farming Squares. A total monopoly," Ma explained. "So the Townids all have to grow designated crops decided by the company. And every year they buy soil–"

"What?"

"No!"

"Seriously?"

"That's crazy!"

The family seemed almost more shocked by this than by the earlier revelation of Avril's rule breaking.

"They can't save seeds to plant the next year, because it's against the growing licence," Ma went on.

"Really?" asked Avril. Sam hadn't mentioned this. Ma nodded.

"They showed us the contract before we left. But to be honest, the seeds are probably all F1 hybrids that wouldn't breed true anyway. And they never supply perennials."

"So the Townids are all completely dependent on GreenCult for farming their Squares," mused Uncle David. "And the company is guaranteed an annual income."

"And they arbitrarily increase the prices year on year," added Ma.

David went silent and rubbed his beard.

"When I gave them a few tiny seedlings," Avril butted in, giving Natasha a look that dared her sister to object, "GreenCult came and dug them up, saying it was illegal for anyone to plant non-company crops."

"Which isn't true," said Ma. "It isn't in the contract. And in any case, the family we met seemed pretty sure that an illegality clause like that would be against commercial law, so even if it was in the contract, it wouldn't stand up in court."

"But who cares about court when a massive Agri-Carrier is ripping up your land!" said Avril. "It's not fair!"

"And it isn't our problem!"

Fa had been pacing the kitchen during the discussion between his wife and brother, and now it seemed he couldn't keep quiet any longer.

"Yes, it's unfair! The world isn't fair! And if they know about the valley, they'll want what we have."

"He's right," said Uncle Frank. "It has nothing to do with us. The Townids are their own worst enemies, buying from GreenCult every year–"

"What choice do they have?" Avril was furious. "They're trapped! Their Squares are all they have."

"They're not starving!" Fa came back at her.

"But they're hungry."

Fa stared at her. Avril held his gaze.

"They eat this disgusting watered-down porridge."

"Porridge!" Little Lexie piped up excitedly from

Grandma's knee, and Avril flashed the toddler a smile before ploughing on.

"And vitamin supplements. The fresh rations aren't adequate. They're taking pills to ward off diseases – like scurvy! Everyone's desperate to grow anything they can."

Fa was staring at Avril, his eyes unreadable.

She tried to find the words to convince everyone. "You say we can't interact with them because they'll want what we have – why shouldn't they? Why should we have so much and they have nothing? How is that okay?"

Fa opened his mouth to speak, but Uncle David got there first, standing up.

"It does seem unfair."

"It doesn't just seem, it is!" said Avril. "And we–"

"And we have the power to do something about it," Uncle David finished calmly.

Everyone looked up at him.

"We could help," he said.

Fa stared at his brother. "I thought you were on my side."

"Why do there need to be sides, Josh?"

Uncle David looked at the family crowded around the big table. Avril followed his gaze and saw her siblings leaning forward in their seats. Natasha's hands were clasped in such a tight knot that her knuckles were white.

"I've been meaning to talk to you for a while," Uncle

David said to Fa slowly. "Some of the family are starting to feel that it's time to broaden our horizons."

"What?"

"Go beyond the valley. We can't hide away forever."

"Have you lost your mind? First, you're talking about helping total strangers in town – people who might be the ones who raided us. Who destroyed everything and left us hungry. Who gave me this scar!"

Fa ran a hand over the ridged line on his skull.

"And now you're saying we should all go skipping out into the world, telling everyone where we live! We might as well put up a sign saying, 'free food here'!"

"You know that's not what I mean."

Avril wondered how much effort it was costing Uncle David to keep his voice so steady.

"The kids are suffocating," he finished quietly.

There was a tense pause as the two brothers stared at each other across the table. Fa was the first to break it.

"You weren't here the winter we went hungry."

"But I came to help as soon as you asked. I'm here now."

"And now you want to leave the valley, to put us all in danger!" Fa's rage exploded. "I'm having no part in it! This is on your head, David. If you bring a raid on us, I will never forgive you."

The door slammed behind him, leaving a swirl of dust motes in the air and an uneasy silence.

Uncle David turned to Ma. "Is Avril right? Do the Townids want teaching?"

"Yes." Ma nodded. "They were very insistent that they didn't want handouts. They just wanted information."

"And they need it! They use poison on the land!" said Avril, remembering elderly Mr Trigg watching masked neighbours spray his Square.

There were gasps from around the table.

"I can believe it," said Ma. "They're so reliant on GreenCult – buying soil, fertiliser, planting what they're told when they're told – that they have no idea how to make compost, improve soil, rotate crops, bring plants back year on year..."

The family were all shaking their heads in varying degrees of sorrow or disbelief. Avril felt – not for the first time – like a blackbird in a flock of chickens. How was it possible that every single one of her relatives found compost more interesting than, oh, anything else in the whole world?

"But the risk!" said Uncle Frank.

"Yes," said Grandma. "We've worked so hard to restore things since the raid."

"It would be short-sighted of them," said Uncle David, "to take one season of food instead of a lifetime of knowledge–"

Uncle Frank interrupted him with a snort of impatience.

"Yes, but people are short-sighted when they're desperate!"

"If they're desperate, isn't that all the more reason to help them?" Avril exclaimed, and was gratified to see Uncle David nodding in his slow, considered way.

"I want to help!" said Natasha. "I've been studying. Since I had to leave uni, I've tried to keep learning. I could teach people."

"I haven't," said Ben cheekily, "but I'll help."

"Even Ben could teach people who have zero knowledge," said Dustin, prodding his brother in the ribs.

"We all know more than we realise, just from working in the valley," said Uncle David. "I think anyone who wants to help would be able to offer something useful."

"Hang on a minute!" Uncle Frank's face was red. "Are you seriously going to do this? Against our wishes?"

Uncle David sighed. "What do you think?" he said, turning to his father.

Grandpa was looking pale and tired. Avril almost felt guilty for causing him stress, until she heard his answer.

"I think those who want to help should do so."

"What!" said Uncle Frank.

"With conditions!" Grandpa hastened to add. "No-one must reveal the location of Home Valley or give anyone clues about how to get here."

"Avril's already blown that secret!" exclaimed Ben.

"Butt out, Ben!" Avril retorted.

"Quiet!" said Ma sharply. "The Townid boy doesn't know the way through the tunnels."

"And anyway, I trust him!"

"Trust no-one," said Grandpa, sounding like Fa. "Go carefully. Be cautious. Reveal nothing. Offer a few talks, workshops. See what the response is. David, you must continually assess the safety of the situation. If you have any doubts, stop."

"Agreed," said Uncle David. "We'll observe total secrecy. Got that, everyone?"

Avril nodded vigorously and saw her siblings and older cousins doing the same.

Uncle David turned to Uncle Frank. "On these conditions, can you agree to us doing this?"

Uncle Frank wore a sceptical expression, but reluctantly nodded, and Aunt Jodi followed suit.

"That's what we'll do then," said Uncle David. "We'll travel discreetly to town, meet the Townid family and offer a set of permaculture workshops. They can invite friends and neighbours, and we'll see how it goes." He surveyed the room with a serious expression. "I promise we won't jeopardise the family home."

Lexie put up her small, pudgy hand and waved it in the air.

"What is it, darling?" Uncle David smiled at his daughter. "Do you want to join in?"

"I want porridge!"

Everyone laughed much more than they would normally, the tension in the room dissipating as the moment of decision-making passed.

"I'm not surprised," said David's wife, Nessa. "It's long past breakfast time."

"Porridge it is!" said David. "Let's go home."

Chairs scraped as everyone stood, preparing to leave and get on with their days.

"You lot." Uncle David addressed Avril's siblings and cousins over the bustle. "Join us for breakfast? We can talk things over, devise a plan?"

"Okay," said Natasha. "We'll follow you over."

Avril helped her stack away some of the extra chairs while Dustin and Ben cleared the mugs from the table.

Uncle David was talking quietly to Ma. "What about you, Sophie? Will you help in the town?"

"I can't say yet." Ma's voice was full of tension. "I need to talk to Josh."

"Understood," Uncle David said. "He always was a stubborn one. I hope he'll come round."

Lexie toddled across the floor and Uncle David swung her high in the air, making her giggle loudly.

"Come on," said Nessa from the doorway, little

Christo holding her hand. "Let's go put the porridge on!"

Uncle David and Nessa left, followed by Natasha, Ben and Dustin. Avril felt a surge of excitement. It was happening! They were going to help – and she'd be able to see Sam again. She went quickly towards the front door.

"Avril!"

She froze and looked at Ma.

"Yes?"

"Stop right there. You won't be going out this week."

"What?"

"Whatever the others may have decided about helping those Townids, the fact remains that you deliberately disobeyed our rules. Fa and I can't ignore that. You'll be spending the next seven days in your room."

Avril inhaled with shock. She was about to protest when she caught her mum's eye. Ma's face was stony. Avril left the room in silence, ran up the stairs and flung herself onto her bed.

Half an hour later, there was a knock at the door. Ma came in with a plate of bread and jam.

"Breakfast."

"Thanks."

Ma took the deskscreen from Avril's desk and tucked it under her arm.

"Really?"

"Sorry. And I'm going to have to lock the door."

"What! Don't you trust me?"

"Well, considering recent behaviour – no."

Avril buried a scream in her pillow.

"I think it's probably a good thing for you to be up here, out of Fa's way for a few days." Ma gave wry smile. "He'll calm down, but right now you're not his favourite person."

She went to the door. "Do you have enough books? Do you need a craft activity?"

"I'm fine," said Avril, her voice muffled.

"Okay, I'll bring you some lunch later."

The door closed and Avril heard the ker-click of a key being turned in the lock.

She lay on the bed in a state of humid fury, until the pre-dawn escape and journey to town caught up with her and she fell into a deep sleep.

NINE

Sam

"Soil is alive," said Natasha.

She sounded like a conjurer, revealing a secret and fantastical spell. Sam stood with the assorted group of neighbours and townspeople in the park, wondering why Avril's sister had brought the family rubbish bin to a growing workshop. He'd attended the event in the hope of seeing Avril, but there was no sign of her, and now he was staring at a large tub full of vegetable scraps and shredded cardboard. There was a row of similar containers set out on a trestle table, and Natasha was removing the lids as she spoke.

"In one square metre of soil there could be half a million tiny, living organisms."

"Like worms?" said next-door neighbour Bridget.

"Well, yes, definitely worms, but also smaller things – I'm talking microbes. Bacteria, fungi, protozoa!" said Natasha.

"Oh," said Bridget, sounding intimidated.

A few people in the group exchanged wary glances.

"It sounds scientific, but it's not complicated," Natasha reassured them. "Microbes are microscopic creatures that work together to create intricate biological architectures. They make nutrients in the soil available to plants."

"Which is why we need to buy it from Green-Cult," said the bike repair mechanic.

"No!" said Natasha. "Come to the table and look. Move from one end to another, so you can see into each tub."

Everyone crowded round and shuffled along the table, peering at the display, while Natasha described what they were looking at.

"At this end is the tub we keep on the counter in our kitchen. You can see yesterday's potato and carrot peelings from supper, apple cores, torn-up cardboard and so on. Every day or two, we empty the kitchen tub onto the compost heap. In the other containers along the line, you can see the different stages of compost, as the organic matter decomposes."

"There are worms in this one!" said Bridget from the middle of the row, sounding excited.

"Yep! Worms are the magicians of compost," said Natasha. "They transform our scraps by shredding them, breaking everything down and aerating the compost pile with their burrowing."

Sam stood next to Bridget and stared into one of the containers. Slender pink worms curled slowly through the miniature mountain of cabbage leaves, grass clippings and ripped paper. Their curving movements reminded him of the treble clef in music. He remembered the fat earthworm that had crawled from his palm onto Avril's, and glanced around for the hundredth time, wishing she'd shown up at the workshop.

"As well as kitchen scraps," Natasha continued, "we also add clippings from the garden. Small twigs from pruning, dead flowers, dry leaves and so on. Everything we put in the compost adds nutrients."

"Like fertiliser?" asked the bike mechanic.

"Yes, but not artificial – not the stuff GreenCult sells. Their fertilisers are synthetic – they make them from fossil fuels!"

Sam was dumbfounded. Fossil fuels? His parents had always aspired to buy fertiliser for improving growth on the family Square. Everyone knew fossil fuels drove climate change – the world had switched to renewable energy because of it – so how come no-one had noticed GreenCult were still selling fossil fuel products? If compost was the answer, he'd better pay attention to the workshop. He dragged his focus back to what Natasha was saying.

"Plants are like humans, right? They need food and water. So, you know how fruit and vegetables are good for our health?"

"Uh-huh," said the bike mechanic.

"Well, what's good for us is good for plants. Like, for instance, we need potassium–"

"Do we?"

Natasha looked a touch exasperated. "Yes, we do! So, the potassium in avocados is healthy for us, and by adding the skins to the compost heap we're giving potassium to the plants."

"I've never had an avocado," said Bridget, expressing the thought in Sam's head.

The nods of agreement around them suggested they weren't the only ones.

"I thought they only grew abroad?" Bridget added. "You can't get them here?"

Natasha's expression seemed almost guilty.

"They never used to grow in this country," she said. "But we have a sheltered spot. And my grandpa says growing conditions are different these days because of climate change."

There was a glum pause at the thought of global heating, interrupted by a new voice floating over the crowd.

"Don't forget the human mineral contribution!"

"Dustin!" Natasha didn't look happy to see her brother. "I thought you were at the shops."

"Yeah, finished. Aren't you going to tell your students about the easiest way to get nitrogen into their compost?"

There was a rustle of curiosity from the group. Natasha went pink.

"You've got your propagation workshop to run, don't interfere in mine!"

"What my sister is embarrassed to tell you," Dustin grinned mightily, "is that human urine is a great way of getting nitrogen into compost! Have a pee, stir with a stick, job done."

There were smiles from the crowd.

"My brothers and I regularly wee on our compost heap," Dustin went on. "And I promise you, I have the best aim!"

Bridget giggled.

"It's a bit trickier for our sisters. But honestly–"

"Shut up, Dustin!" Natasha was bright red. "That's more than enough information. And this is my workshop! Butt out!"

"Sorry."

Dustin didn't sound apologetic at all. He sauntered off and sat on the ground, long legs outstretched. Natasha turned her back on him and tried to regain her composure.

"So, you've seen the stages of the composting process. The worms working their magic. And when the compost is ready, like this sample here, you spread it on the earth." She took the lid off the final container. "And here's the result: rich, fertile soil!"

Sam recognised the contents – it was what Avril had brought in her makeshift sled.

"This is nothing like what we've been buying!" said Bridget. "Can I touch it?"

"Yes, go ahead," said Natasha. "That's the point. GreenCult have been selling you such poor-quality soil it's practically dirt."

"What's the different between dirt and soil?" someone asked in a timid voice.

"Dirt is dead," said Natasha, her expression fierce. "Soil is a living ecosystem. Dirt will never sustain life. And GreenCult's way of farming is turning more of the earth into dirt every year."

Sam could see her anger reflected in the faces around him. The silence felt depressed, until Natasha lightened the atmosphere.

"Compost is free to make and one of the key ways of transforming dirt into living soil. By adding compost to your Squares, you'll improve the soil year on year. You'll never need to buy it again!"

People pressed closer to the table in excited response to this extraordinary statement. As Natasha continued her talk, Sam moved along to let every-one have a good view. Something bright pink in his peripheral vision stopped him. He stepped away from the display.

It was Avril.

In the ten days that had passed since their dawn

assignation, Sam had started to wonder if she would ever come to town again. She hadn't messaged once, and he'd begun to doubt if she even liked him in the first place. Maybe she'd had enough of coming to Newbeck. Maybe he'd done something wrong. Maybe she hadn't liked the way he kissed.

And now here she was, strolling in the sunshine towards the gathering, casual and relaxed, as if she came here every day.

The sight of her now made him feel excited and anxious and somehow angry. Why hadn't she been in touch? Was she ignoring him? But he also felt his skin tingle at the sight of her. Under the brim of her vivid hat, her unbrushed hair crackled around her pale face. He wanted to smooth it with his palm just to feel the straw texture against her soft skin.

He took a step forward and she spotted him, her face lighting up. Sam felt a matching glow inside himself as she approached.

"Hi," he said.

"Hi," she beamed. "I've just been to the school, hoping I'd see you."

She stood next to him and the back of her hand brushed against his. He was about to speak when Natasha called for silence and Avril leaned close to whisper. "We need to stay quiet. My sister will kill me if I interrupt."

Her breath tickled his ear.

Sam nodded, then whispered back. "You okay?"

Avril nodded and put her finger to her lips.

Now, Sam couldn't concentrate on soil improvement. He waited while Natasha continued to talk about mulching and no-dig techniques. People kept asking questions and Sam began to get impatient. How much longer would it take? What if Avril had to leave straight after the talk? He was supposed to be taking the fresh rations home before weeding the family Square. He couldn't stand around all afternoon.

Eventually, Natasha wrapped things up. "Okay, we'd better stop there. Thanks for coming."

There was an outburst of applause, and people clustered around her, eager to ask more questions.

"This has been a revelation! Thank you!" said Bridget. "Will you be doing more? Please say yes!"

While Natasha was distracted, Sam and Avril drifted a little way from the group.

"So..." Sam didn't know how to frame all the questions buzzing in his head, and ended saying lamely, "You okay?"

"Just glad to be out!" Avril said. "My parents locked me in my room for a week."

Sam grimaced sympathy. "Harsh."

"Yeah. And without my deskcreen, so I couldn't message you!"

He felt a flicker of relief that she had wanted to contact him, that she hadn't deliberately cut him off.

"Since they let me out two days ago, I've been on

garden duty and extra chores. Ma's barely let me out of her sight. Talk about the valley prison!"

An image of Home Valley flashed into Sam's mind, the lush green fields and white apple blossoms.

"Didn't think I'd be able to come to town again for ages. I begged and begged Natasha, and she said if it was okay with Fa, I could tag along. When I asked, he just grunted, so I took it as a yes. Skipped lunch to get my farm chores done in time and here I am!"

Sam frowned. Skipped lunch? Voluntarily?

"Have you been at school today?" Avril chattered on. "You're so lucky! I was daydreaming in my room for hours last week, trying to imagine what it must be like. So wonderful, to–"

"Wonderful?" interrupted Sam.

At midday break, Caldo and Marley had knocked half his meagre food onto the floor and stepped on it so he couldn't even retrieve it. Then Clifford the caretaker had yelled at him for making a mess. He'd been so hungry he couldn't focus during the circular economics test and had been told off by the tutor for failing when he'd spent all weekend studying.

"Yes, wonderful!" said Avril. "To see people you aren't related to every day! To have the freedom to go to school, study different subjects, play team games–"

"The only game I've been playing is dodge the bullies!" said Sam bitterly. "There's no freedom at school. You don't know what you're talking about."

"Well, you've got more freedom than me!"

"Oh, really? Yeah, I'm so free – free to weed the Square, collect the rations! Free to be told off and called names and–"

"We haven't been allowed to leave the valley for four years!" Avril interjected hotly.

"Why would you want to leave the valley! If you knew what it's like to be hungry every day, you wouldn't be so keen on your mythical idea of freedom. You live in this beautiful place full of food and all you do is moan about it!"

"A place where I'm completely trapped! My future set in stone, every tree in the orchard another bar on my cage–"

"At least they grow fruit! See this bag? That's the week's rations for my whole family. You're so selfish!"

Avril opened her mouth to retort when her sister interrupted them with a shout.

"Avril! Time to go."

Sam and Avril stared at each other, eyes snapping; hers were dark as evergreen leaves, his like wet soil.

Avril turned on her heel and stalked away, climbing into the small electric vehicle beside her sister without a backward look.

TEN

Avril

Avril was so angry she could hardly hear what Natasha was saying as her sister drove them back to Home Valley.

"... they seemed really receptive, lots to learn of course, but keen – and that's the main thing. You have to want to know..."

"Uh-huh."

"And isn't it just heaven to be somewhere differ-ent!" Natasha sighed with pleasure.

"Exactly!" Avril exclaimed. "Exactly!"

Fa was waiting for them at the driveway barrier, a glowering expression on his face.

"You're late."

"Sorry," said Natasha, sounding not at all repentant. "Everyone had so many questions!"

"Avril, help with the branches please," he said, ignoring Natasha's apology. "You can come back with me in the tractor. Natasha, Ma needs you in the greenhouse."

Avril climbed out of the car resentfully and watched Natasha squeeze the small vehicle through the gap beside the horizontal tree trunk. When the car had whirred away, Fa used the tractor and a rope to drag the barrier back into place. Avril and Fa spent the next twenty minutes piling armfuls of branches over and around it to make the way look impassable.

"Not too tidy!" Fa criticised Avril's work. "It needs to look natural."

Avril kept her mouth shut. She suspected the job was a form of punishment, Fa trying to make a point about how wrong he thought it was for anyone to leave the valley.

Eventually, he was satisfied with how it looked and gestured for her to climb into the little electric tractor. Avril stared out the window as they drove towards the farmhouse, replaying the argument with Sam, her fury ebbing and starting to mingle with other emotions.

"Avril? Avril!"

She realised Fa had been talking to her.

"Did you hear a word I just said?"

"Um–" Avril considered lying, but suspected it would lead to more trouble. "Sorry, I was thinking."

"Careful, you might pull a muscle!"

It was one of Fa's oldest jokes, and on good days she'd give him a token smile for effort, but now her face felt stuck.

Avril expected him to pull up at the house, but instead he drove straight past and pulled onto the track leading up to the far fields.

"Hang on! Can I get out?" said Avril.

"I need your help fixing one of the wind turbines," said Fa. "That's what you missed when you were thinking."

"Oh."

Avril gritted her teeth.

Neither of them spoke as the tractor bumped along the track and they pulled up at the top end of the valley. Fa was never much of a talker, and today Avril was glad of the silence, keeping her words to a minimum as they approached the group of wind turbines.

"Which one?"

"Here," said Fa, leading her to one near the middle of the group. "There was an alert this morning. Sensors detected a problem."

Avril opened the taskpad in the trunk of the turbine and tapped at the screen. A quick scan revealed a minuscule crack in one of the propeller tips. She programmed the maintenance bot for a repair and watched the little domed machine scuttle upwards towards the slowly revolving blades.

"Sorted," she said. "It'll be fixed in ten."

"Good," said Fa. "Knew you'd be quicker with the tech than me."

He leaned against the base of the wind turbine and looked out across the valley. Avril followed his example, her gaze travelling over the green curves of land to the wooden farmhouse, small in the distance. At that moment, she hated all of it.

"Beautiful," said Fa.

Avril's jaw was stone.

"Isn't it?" Fa pushed her.

She shrugged.

"What's up?"

She didn't answer. After a minute, he said, "I let you go, didn't I?" His voice grew in irritation. "I still think this whole business is a crazy risk to take. But the family's gone against me and I'm letting it happen. You went to town with Natasha and I didn't stop you. I didn't say anything. And now you're ignoring me!"

"I'm not!"

"Well, it sure as hell feels like it!"

Avril blinked, feeling the sting of tears in her eyes. Sam's angry face flashed into her mind. She clenched her jaw.

"I'm upset about something else."

Fa's voice softened. "What is it?"

Avril looked at the familiar weathered face and knew he wouldn't understand, but equally that he cared. She tried to give him something he could grasp.

"That boy, the Townid, I thought... I thought we were friends. I thought he got me, you know? But we had this horrible argument today. He was mean. And he just didn't care how I felt. All he could talk about was how lucky I am to have enough to eat." She gestured to the view. "To live in a 'beautiful place full of food'."

Fa's forehead crinkled with a frown that almost reached the bald expanse of his head. "He's right, isn't he?"

"What?"

"We are lucky."

Avril felt a tear spill onto her cheek and trickle towards her chin. "Yes, but..."

He waited for her to finish the sentence, but now the tears were coming thick and fast.

"But what, Avril? Why don't you feel lucky?"

Fa's voice was so sad and full of concern that Avril found herself crying even harder.

"Because... because... I feel trapped!" she managed to blurt out.

"Ahh," Fa exhaled slowly. He lowered himself to the ground and sat on the grass, his back against the trunk of the turbine, knees bent. Avril sat cross-legged beside him. After a minute, Fa said, "It's what Uncle David was talking about, isn't it?"

Avril nodded and wiped her face again.

"You do know why we decided to hide ourselves and the location of the valley?"

"The raid," Avril said dully.

"To protect you. Because... when they attacked... I couldn't stop them."

Avril was shocked to hear a crack in Fa's voice. She watched his hands become fists on his knees.

"The way they smashed everything – they could've hurt you. And I was powerless."

Avril remembered seeing Fa unconscious, blood on his head, his face grey. Uncle David had struggled to drag him into the farmhouse and Fa's arms had splayed out, limp, as if he were dead.

"That winter, seeing you all go hungry..." he went on, "I never want to live through that again. It ate me up. Relying on rations, seeing my own children going without food."

Avril remembered what Sam had said and felt lacerated with guilt. He'd said he was hungry every day. She remembered the porridge the family had offered her, and how she hadn't even eaten it. She suddenly realised why the orange pill had tasted familiar. They had taken vitamins during those long months after the raid, when they'd been forced to depend on government rations.

"But that's how it is every day for the Townids!" she burst out. "They are always hungry."

Fa nodded.

"So, we must help them!" she said.

"I don't know," said Fa heavily. "I just don't know."

That night, when Avril climbed the darkened stairs with a glass of water, she heard the rumble of lowered voices in Ma and Fa's bedroom. She stopped on the landing and tried to hear what was being said, but could only make out a few words. She crept closer and pressed her back against the wall beside the closed door.

"You really want to take the risk? You think David's right?" Fa's voice rose above its previous whisper.

"I don't know who's right!" Ma exclaimed. Her next words were quieter but still audible. "It is a risk. I recognise that. But the way Natasha describes it, the Townids are desperate to learn. None of them have asked for so much as a handful of seeds, just her time."

"I wasn't happy about today."

"Natasha's twenty-four, Josh. She's an adult. It's her choice."

"She took Avril! Who is still a child."

"Why didn't you forbid it when they asked?"

There was a deep silence and Avril pressed her ear to the wooden wall, hoping they hadn't started whispering. Then she heard Fa clearing his throat.

"I didn't know what to do," he said, his voice husky. "I don't know what to do. I used to know. And David always agreed, but now... Now the family feels divided."

There was a rustling noise. Avril imagined Ma comforting Fa with an embrace, but the image dissolved with his next rough statement.

"And you want to help. You want to join their side."

"There needn't be sides, Josh! I don't want this to cause a rift between us."

"But?"

"But yes. Maybe. Maybe helping feels like a good thing to do."

There was a pause in which Avril could hear Fa's footsteps measuring the length of the bedroom. She could imagine him pacing the room. Ma would be sitting on the bed, trying to maintain her calm as she waited for Fa to process his thoughts. Avril waited too, wondering what he would say.

The footsteps stopped.

"I can't stop you." Fa sounded defeated.

"No!" Ma's voice was vigorous, the way it sounded when she gave the family a pep talk before the most gruelling harvest days. "I'm not having that! Either you support me, or you argue back."

"I told you. I DON'T KNOW!"

Avril held her breath. A long silence followed.

Then a creaking sound as one or both of them sat down.

"Listen, love." Ma was gentle. "Why don't you come with me? The Townids we met, Dexter and Lily, they're organising a community meeting next week. They're worried about a raid."

"WHAT?"

"By GreenCult. They're worried the corporation will come back and destroy things again once the changes become visible. The new way of farming. They're just as scared as we are."

"Huh."

"It would be a good chance for us to meet Dexter and Lily again, get to know them a bit. Meet some of their neighbours, the people who've been attending the talks. Maybe it won't seem so risky if we find out more about them."

Avril waited. She couldn't hear anything. She waited some more, but it didn't seem like Fa was going to respond and her feet were getting cold. Just as she began to tiptoe away, she heard Fa's voice.

"I'll think about it."

ELEVEN

Sam

The Community Arts Space Hall was packed. Sam stood awkwardly at the back with his brother Casey, wishing they weren't the only kids present. He watched his parents greeting people as they arrived – Bridget from next door, the headteacher from school, some shopkeepers he recognised. Sam froze when Caldo and Marley's parents came through the door, but the twins weren't with them.

"I'm bored," said Casey. "We could be at home!"

"Yeah, well." Sam kept his eyes on the door.

He desperately hoped Avril was coming, at the same time not knowing whether he even wanted to see her. It had been ten days since their argument and he'd been thinking about her constantly, vacillating between anger at her selfishness and regret at his own behaviour. He didn't even know whether Avril had been to town. He'd been at school every weekday, and despite attending Growth Workshops at weekends led by each one of her three siblings, he hadn't seen her once.

"But why did you want to come?" Casey badgered him. "It's going to be so boring!"

"Maybe it won't."

Casey huffed and slid down the wall to sit on the floor. Their parents had been pleased at Sam's interest in the community meeting. Sam hadn't predicted they'd bring his brother along too.

"Sam! Casey!"

Their old childminder, Rosie, was approaching, her cheeks living up to her name as she hauled a toddler alongside with her left hand, pushing a buggy with her right. A third infant was strapped to her front in a sling.

"Hi, Rosie," said Sam.

Casey gave her a listless wave from the floor.

The child in the buggy blew a wet raspberry at Sam. Rosie ignored it.

"Your parents said you were here!" she said breathlessly. "I want to attend the meeting. But there's no way I can keep the kids quiet for long enough."

For a horrendous moment, Sam thought she was going to ask him to babysit three toddlers.

"Can you take notes for me?"

He was so relieved he agreed at once. "Yes, sure."

"Oh fantastic, thank you. I've asked them to do an audio recording, but the quality isn't always great when lots of people speak over each other in different parts of the room. So, I'd really appreciate it if you could jot down the key points and bring them round later. Talk me through it?"

It was starting to feel like a homework assignment, but when Sam heard bubbling sounds coming from the buggy-toddler's nappy area, he decided he'd got off lightly.

"Sure," he said. "Are you mainly interested in the Growth Workshop stuff?"

"Oh, no!" said Rosie. "I mean, I try, of course I do. But when you're childminding ten or twelve hours a day, it's almost impossible to keep on top of a Square. I'm so tired by the evening, and of course at the weekends I'm helping out with the grandkids."

Sam crinkled his forehead. "So basically, you're always nappy-changing?"

Rosie laughed – a tired kind of sound. "It's different with the grandkids! I love spending time with them. But since Jason – well, I just haven't been able to get our Square to be very productive."

Sam had vague memories of Rosie's husband, Jason. He'd also been smiley and red-cheeked, and used to throw Sam in the air if he came home early from work. Sam remembered his parents' solemn faces when they'd told him Jason had died and that "Rosie might be a bit sad sometimes". He'd never really thought about it before, but it came to him now that he and his family were lucky to have four of them to farm their Square. It sounded as though Rosie had to rely on rations alone. How many other people in Newbeck were in the same situation?

"No, I wanted to attend the meeting because of the rumours," Rosie went on, automatically retrieving a spat-out dummy and mopping a dribbly chin as she spoke. "Everyone's saying GreenCult might come. I want to know what the plan is. I want to support the community."

"Ohhh, right. Sure," Sam said. "No problem."

"Because I love the changes." Rosie was fumbling in one of several bags hanging from the buggy. "Like the wild grasses starting to grow on the verges, now the council's stopped that stupid mowing. And two new saplings in my street. It's lovely – aha! Here!" Rosie shoved a small notebook at him. "And... Oh, where's that pencil?"

She located it in the grip of the infant strapped to her chest and, extricating it from the small chubby fist, handed it over. The pencil was chewed and still slightly wet.

"Thanks," said Sam.

"You're a star, Sam! Thank you so much!"

"No problem." Sam discreetly wiped the pencil on his trousers.

"Say bye-bye, say bye-bye." Rosie made two of the toddlers wave at Sam. "Say bye-bye!"

The one in the buggy blew another raspberry.

"Bye, Casey! Bye, Sam!"

"Er, bye," said Sam, as Rosie hurried away.

Sam looked round the room and caught his breath; Avril's mum and dad were coming through the doorway. Josh wore a suspicious expression and scanned the room as if expecting an ambush. Sam watched as Natasha followed them in.

"I'm so **BORED**!"

"Shut up, Casey!"

Sam waited, attention lasered on the entrance. The door slowly swung shut behind Avril's sister and his shoulders sagged. She wasn't coming. He sat on the floor beside Casey.

"What's with you?" said his brother.

"Nothing."

The rows of chairs were becoming crowded, and the hall was almost full when Sam's mum went to stand in the clear patch of floor at the front that served as a stage and raised her hands for quiet. She spoke towards the microphone.

"Er, hello, everyone. Can you hear me?"

"No!" bellowed someone at the back.

"Is that better?" She moved closer to the mic.

"Yes!"

There were a few titters of laughter and Mum smiled. She seemed confident, but Sam suspected she was hiding nerves under the surface.

"Okay, good! Thank you, everyone, for coming.

And thank you, particularly, to the Fairburns."

There was a smattering of applause and everyone looked at Avril's family sitting in the front row. Natasha turned and raised a hand to acknowledge the room. Her parents didn't move. Viewed from behind, Josh's immobile head looked like a boulder. Sam wondered what Josh thought of his family helping the townspeople. Judging by his expression as he entered the hall, it didn't seem likely Josh was keen on the project. Why was he even here?

"We are truly so very appreciative of the work you've been doing, sharing your knowledge and expertise with the Newbeck community," Mum said. "The growth programme is already making a difference in our Squares and on our streets."

"Hear hear!" the school headteacher called out.

"But the visibility of this difference makes it a danger," Mum said. "My husband and I have direct experience of how GreenCult can react to anything that challenges their monopoly. We planted a few small seedlings–"

I planted them actually, Sam thought grumpily, jotting some notes in Rosie's pad.

"– and they brought an AgriCarrier with two armed guards to tear up the soil and plants, claiming – falsely – we had gone against their contract."

Sam was pretty sure everyone in town had already heard the story, but the mutters of shock and dissatisfaction that rumbled round the room made it sound like dramatic news.

"We don't even know how they found out about the planting," Mum went on. "Which leads us to believe they're monitoring us somehow."

"Er..."

Sam was surprised to see their next-door neighbour, Bridget, tentatively raise her hand.

"Yes, Bridget?"

"I'm so sorry, really I am, but – well, I think it might have been me..."

"What?" Mum forgot to speak into the microphone, but her expression made it obvious what she was saying.

"I'm so sorry!" Bridget had gone red in the face and was sounding slightly tearful. "When I saw your seedlings, well, I just assumed they must be from GreenCult. I thought there must be extra crop options that I'd somehow missed out on. And when I saw you had strawberry plants–"

There was a murmur of longing from some of the crowd at the thought of strawberries.

"– well, I messaged them."

"You contacted GreenCult?" Mum was incredulous.

"Yes. I asked for some strawberry plants. And when they said strawberries weren't on this year's approved list, I told them that they must be, since my neighbour had two seedlings in their Square."

"Oh."

"Idiot."

Bridget flinched at the insult that shot from the crowd. It was impossible to be certain, but Sam was fairly sure the attack came from Caldo and Marley's family.

"I didn't mean for the plants to be destroyed!" Bridget glared at the rows of faces and Sam noticed a few people avoiding her eye. "And I didn't have to own up, did I? I'm doing the right thing, so have some respect! I'm only telling you now because I didn't want everyone to think the corporation has secret cameras or spies or something!"

"Thank you, Bridget," said Mum, regaining her composure. "We really appreciate your honesty."

"And the fact is–" Sam's dad stepped forward to the mic, "– it's entirely possible someone who hasn't attended the workshops might make the same assumption. Or a visitor from another town."

"Quite right!" Bridget said, as she plumped back into her seat.

"And the more obvious it becomes that we're planting non-approved crops," Dad went on, "growing trees and allowing wildflowers to flourish on verges, the more likely it is that they'll send the guards to crush our progress."

"But we won't let them!" bellowed the local artist, Denley Emmitt, sounding delighted by the prospect of a fight.

"Exactly!" said Mum. "We're here today to agree a plan for how we can stand strong against Green-Cult whenever it may try to take action against us."

"How?" said a shopkeeper.

"I don't know," Mum admitted. "But if we don't find a way, then all our new growth work will be wasted."

"You said the guards were armed?" The shopkeeper sounded deeply alarmed.

"Only with truncheons and scowls!" Mum replied firmly. "And we have strength in numbers."

"Let me at them! Those–" yelled Denley Emmitt, following up with a string of colourful curses before he was shushed by the people sitting near him.

The headteacher spoke up. "We need an early-warning system. If we know they're coming, maybe we can talk to them before they smash anything."

"Roadcams!" said the chief of the town's two-person police force. "We monitor traffic in and out of town. Not that there is much. We can use those..." He hesitated. "As long as you're sure the Growth Programme isn't illegal? What if GreenCult is right?"

"I can promise you," said Mum. "I've been through the contract with tweezers and they've got nothing on us."

The policeman looked doubtful, then decided. "Okay. We'll need volunteers if we're to keep watch twenty-four-seven."

"I can do nights," called out the school caretaker, Clifford, then explained to the people near him, "Insomnia."

"And me!"

"I'll do a shift."

Several voices called out from around the hall.

Sam's mum grabbed her handscreen. "This is a good start," she said. "We can draw up a rota."

She left the stage area and began collecting names on the screen.

"I'll do triple shifts if someone can farm my Square," said elderly Mr Trigg.

Sam remembered Avril's reaction when they saw Mr Trigg's neighbours spraying his land with weed-killer. A thought started to thrum in his brain.

"And me!" shouted someone else.

"Nah, I'd rather weed than stare at roadcams for hours!" came a different voice.

"Same!"

People began to chatter among themselves, sharing their opinions and commenting on the action of the meeting so far. Sam scribbled key points in the notebook, and his thoughts turned to Rosie. Her Square had been neglected since her husband died. Mr Trigg couldn't farm even a tiny part of his Square. The Growth Programme wasn't going to help either of them very much, but Rosie had still wanted to be part of the community plan against GreenCult.

The thoughts were like an insistent rhythm demanding attention. Sam hesitated, but the idea was too loud to ignore.

"I'll be back in a sec," he said to Casey, pocketing the notepad.

Sam squeezed along the crowded back wall, trying to avoid stepping on feet – excuse me, excuse me – until he managed to get to the side of the room and navigate along the edge to the front of the rows of chairs.

"Dad," he hissed, standing by the small stage area. "Dad!"

Dad was standing near the mic, waiting while the rota sign-ups happened. He came over to Sam.

"What is it?"

"Listen, the Squares system is stupid."

"Not now, Sam, this really isn't the time for a political–"

"No, it's exactly the time!" Sam was surprised at his own vehemence. "Rosie can't manage her Square. There are probably loads of people who can't. So, they go without fresh food and all that growing space goes to waste. If we're having a rota to watch road-cams, why don't we have a farming rota too? Share out tasks that play to people's strengths!"

Dad stared at him. Sam stared back. After an immense pause, during which the noisy chatter of the crowd seemed somehow very far away, Dad spoke. "You might be onto something."

"Yes!"

"It'll take a heck of a lot of organising."

"Yeah. But this is the time to try, right? When everyone's here."

Dad strode forward to the microphone and spoke into it.

"Quiet, everyone! Quiet please!"

The room stuttered into silence. Everyone waited, and for a moment Dad seemed to struggle for words. Sam felt nervous on his behalf.

Then Dad spoke. "Since we're collecting names for a rota, I wonder if we might consider something more ambitious."

A sea of curious faces gazed at him.

"Why don't we share out other tasks too? Because the Squares system... Let's face it... It doesn't really work, does it?"

"Works just fine for us!" the twins' mum called out. "But I guess if you don't put the effort in–"

A hubbub swelled as people talked among themselves, raising their voices in a confusion of reactions.

"She's got a point."

"That's ridiculous–"

"What an unfair thing to say–"

"He's right!"

"He's mad!"

"This isn't what we came here for!"

"Listen, please..." Dad was trying to get the room to hush but no-one was paying attention.

Sam felt blood rushing to his face and hoped his Dad wasn't feeling the same humiliation.

"QUIET!"

An unamplified voice boomed through the room. Sam was astonished to realise it was Avril's dad, Josh. Everyone fell silent.

"LISTEN to the man!"

"Er... Thanks. Um..."

Sam willed Dad to convince them. The silence was restless. Mum made her way back to the stage area and gave Dad an encouraging nod. He began to speak, slowly.

"What I mean is... We each have the same land. But we're not all great at using it. Some of us can't."

"That's true!" called out Mr Trigg.

"We've just agreed to run a rota to monitor road-cams, right?"

There was scattered nodding.

"So why don't we share out other tasks, too? Like weeding and planting and harvesting?"

"Too lazy to farm your own land?" someone shouted.

"No, I mean, why aren't we all making the most of our strengths? Doing the tasks we're best suited to?" Dad continued, his voice hesitant. "Grubbing away on individual Squares doesn't make sense. Especially now there's the chance to grow more than just four crops."

"So we should all work ten times as hard, should

we?" called out the twins' dad. "We have day jobs, you know!"

"No! That's not..." Dad was drowned out again as a grumbling murmur filled the room.

"I'm not weeding someone else's Square!"

"I've got enough to do!"

"He's insane!"

Sam closed his eyes for a second. The idea wasn't clear enough. They weren't getting it. How could Dad get through to them?

"SQUARES ARE RIDICULOUS."

Sam's eyes snapped open. Josh was standing up and glaring ferociously at the crowd.

"The GreenCult monopoly is a disgrace. The idea of only growing authorised crops is a nonsense."

Josh spoke with such authority that everyone in the room was silent and listening.

"If my family are set on helping you, the least you can do is help yourselves! On our farm, we don't take a field each and work it individually – that would be madness! We work together. And we each have key skills. Composting, propagation, carpentry, pruning, grafting, tech, seed saving and so on. Natasha tends the greenhouse. Ben the trees. Dustin the compost. Sophie plans the crop rotations. Avril does the computing."

"What do YOU do?" called out a cheeky voice.

Sam held his breath. How would Josh react to the provocation? He watched Avril's mum put a hand on her husband's arm and felt the air tense around them.

"Me?" Josh made everyone wait as he surveyed the room. "Me? I just boss everyone around."

There was a ripple of uncertain laughter at the unexpected joke. Sam was dumbfounded. Josh had a sense of humour?

Josh waited for silence to return.

"You don't have to listen to me," he said. "I'm not part of this. But a community initiative to draw on people's strengths makes perfect sense. It'll be complicated to organise. Yeah, there'll be teething problems. But is it worth a try? I think you'd be mad not to."

He scanned the crowd as if daring people to challenge him, then abruptly sat down. There was utter silence. Sam could feel everyone thinking.

Then the owner of the Repair Workshop spoke up. "I hate weeding, but I'll build an irrigation system for anyone's Square!"

"I quite like weeding," said Bridget quietly.

"There you go!" said Dad, his face lit up with relief. "If we shared the work, we could share the harvest. We might end up with more for everyone."

"I could deliver produce!" called out the young man who ran the bike-servicing stall. "My bike has a trailer."

There was a hum of chatter as everyone in the hall considered the idea. Sam watched as different groups variously nodded or disagreed with each other as they supported or opposed the plan.

"It's a nice thought," the school headteacher said loudly, getting the attention of the room, "but very complicated. I think it might be too difficult to organise."

"I can do spreadsheets," said Mr Trigg, suddenly energised. "I was an accountant."

"It would be incredibly time-consuming," warned the teacher.

"Who cares!" Mr Trigg's craggy face crinkled into a smile. "I'm retired! It'd be better than sitting staring out the window at a neglected patch of land that never produces so much as a bean." He shook a walking stick in the air. "I've got two of these sticks, and a walking frame. I'm no good for gardening. But give me a rota to organise and I can be useful!"

He levered himself to his feet and, leaning at a precarious angle on his sticks, addressed the room. "Who here agrees? Who wants to try?"

A chorus of shouts expressed both agreement and rejection, and hands were raised. It seemed about two-thirds of those present were willing to participate.

"That's enough of us to have a go!" said Mum, clutching the screen and sounding excited. "Let's get a basic road traffic rota going today. We'll work with Mr Trigg–"

"Call me Perce," interrupted the old man, still leaning on his sticks. "Short for Percy."

"We'll work with Perce and make a plan for everything else. Follow-up meeting here, same time next week, to talk it over and start organising. Any questions?"

There were a lot of questions, suggestions, contradictory opinions. Some people drifted out of the hall, having decided not to join the new scheme, but the majority wanted to keep talking. Sam rejoined Casey at the back of the hall and started to scribble notes for Rosie.

"That wasn't as boring as I expected," said Casey. "Denley Emmitt gave me some great new swears."

It took almost an hour for the hall to clear. Sam and Casey were hanging about near the door, waiting for their parents to see off the last stragglers.

"I love it!"

For a second, Sam thought it was Avril speaking and spun round. With a crash of disappointment, he realised it was her sister, Natasha.

"There's something so satisfying about sharing what I know," Natasha enthused to Bridget, walking with her towards the exit. "And to be spending time in different places, meeting new people, exploring ideas together – oh, it's all just wonderful!"

The word pinged like a tuning fork in Sam's brain, chiming with the memory of Avril's angry words. He looked at Natasha and saw that her face was glowing with excitement. Avril wasn't the only one in her family desperate to escape the valley. Sam looked across to where Josh was standing, silent and slightly distant from the group where his wife talked animatedly to Sam's parents. The fact that Avril's dad was in town meant that things were changing in the valley.

Sam just hoped Avril would be allowed back to town soon and, if she was, that she'd still want to speak to him.

TWELVE

Avril

The full family were gathered around the kitchen table once again. Avril was relieved not to be the focus of disapproving attention this time.

"So?" Uncle David expressed the curiosity everyone was feeling. "How was the meeting?"

Ma and Fa looked at each other, but before either could speak Natasha launched into a gabble of excitement.

"Wonderful! It was wonderful! So many people came! And they're lovely, and Dexter had this great idea about a Community Growing Scheme where everyone in town works together, and lots of people want to try it, and we just have to give them some seeds to get them going! Please! We have to!"

"Whoa, slow down!" said Uncle Frank. "What do you mean, a Growing Scheme?"

"It is actually an excellent initiative," said Ma gently, and began to explain things more comprehensibly.

As she listened to Ma's description of the evening, Avril wished she'd been allowed to attend the meeting. Sam's parents had been leading it – maybe he'd even been there with them! She longed to see him. The memory of the fight was like a sore that wouldn't heal; her brain kept scratching it, replaying his words despite the sting.

Natasha's impassioned voice broke through Avril's thoughts.

"... we have more seeds than we're going to use. We've stockpiled extra ever since the raid. It's criminal to keep them in storage when they could be growing and providing food in town."

"Not if we have failed harvests this year!" Uncle Frank protested. "We might need them."

"He's right," said Fa. "We can't rely on having a good year. The weather is more and more unpredictable!"

"If we lose whole crops, we'll need the fallback seeds next year," Frank reiterated.

"True," said Uncle David. "But could we give them some of what we have? Keep some, share some?"

"I'll do a stock assessment," said Natasha eagerly.

"See what we've got. We don't even have accurate records because we've always had such a surplus. I'm sure there'll be some we can spare."

"That's a sensible idea," said Grandpa. "Let's decide once Natasha has assessed what we have in store."

"In the meantime," said Ma, "Is anyone going to volunteer to help with the Community Growing Scheme?"

"Yes!" Several voices spoke at once.

Most of the family put themselves forward: Natasha, Ben, Dustin, Uncle David and Nessa, and the four older cousins.

"I will!" Avril was on her feet with excitement.

Ma went over to the wall where all the valley tasks were listed and uncapped a marker pen. She drew a new box alongside the crop rotation diagrams, wrote "Townid Scheme" as a heading, then listed the volunteers' names beneath.

"We'll have to coordinate," said Ma. "Look at your commitments in the valley and decide how much time you can give. Be realistic!"

"I'll drive to town and sign up today," said Natasha. "Who wants a lift?"

The promised ride was immediately full, and Avril didn't get a place.

"Could I maybe have my bike back?" Avril asked Ma and Fa, trying to sound casual. The bicycle-disguised-as-a-wreck had remained confiscated as part of Avril's punishment, and she hadn't yet dared ask for it back. "Then I can cycle to town myself without bothering anyone for a lift..."

She trailed off at the expression on Fa's face.

"That bike, and our trust, have to be earned," he said, eyebrows drawn together. "I don't want you gadding into town by yourself whenever it takes your fancy. I'll drive you there myself."

Avril stared at the floor, her face hot with humiliation. Everyone else in the family could drive. They were all independent. And none of them would even be going to town if she hadn't gone there in the first place! It was so unfair that she was still being punished.

A week later, Avril's frustration was reaching boiling point.

"Ma, please can you drive me into town?!"

Ma rubbed her forehead and sighed. "Fa said he would, and he will."

"But when? It's been days! Everyone else has been to town. They've all signed up for the Growing Scheme." Avril pointed to the noticeboard-wall. "Look! Tasks!"

"Your turn will come," said Ma, disappearing into the larder.

Avril held back a scream. It had been two weeks

since the argument with Sam and she still winced every time she thought about it. She had to see him.

"I'm trying to do a good thing here!" she said loudly to the larder doorway. "I want to help the Townids turn their lives around! Share my knowledge. And yet–"

Ma reappeared holding a jar of pickles and wearing a sceptical look.

"I'll talk to Fa," said Ma. "Happy?"

"Talk to me about what?"

Fa stood on the kitchen threshold, untying the laces of an extremely muddy pair of boots.

Ma waved her free hand at Avril, shooing her out of the room. Avril retreated to the hallway and leaned against the wall to eavesdrop.

"Josh," said Ma. "Avril's bugging me to go to town."

Avril pursed her lips. Ma wasn't exactly sounding supportive.

"And she's right," Ma went on. "It isn't fair for her to be left out when the other youngsters are all doing it."

There was the double thud of boots hitting the doormat and the scrape of a chair across the floor. Fa didn't say anything. Avril wondered what he was thinking.

After a moment's silence, Ma spoke. "You said you'd take her, but you've been putting it off. What's up?"

Fa sighed.

"Come on, love," said Ma. "Talk to me. It isn't just that you haven't had time, is it?"

"No," Fa's voice rumbled. "I don't want to take her."

Avril clenched her fists in the corridor.

"Why?" asked Ma.

"Don't know," said Fa. "She's the youngest. Maybe it's that. She's more vulnerable than the others."

"But she isn't really," said Ma gently. "She's fifteen. Most kids would have a lot of independence by that age."

"And she hasn't! She's always been here, in the valley. She isn't streetwise!"

"She'll never get streetwise if she isn't allowed out."

Avril dug her fingernails into her palms, willing Fa to hear what Ma was saying.

"And, I guess, I don't know." Fa sounded unusually hesitant. "There's something holding me back. It still doesn't feel right. This whole business with the Townids, the workshops, the growing scheme. It's like everyone's forgotten the raid. You've all just decided to trust a massive group of strangers."

"I think you should talk to Percy Trigg," Ma said decisively. "He knows everyone. He's lived in the town all his life – which is seventy-eight years! And he's in contact with every single person involved in the growing scheme. He's a good egg."

"Huh." Fa sounded unsure.

"Maybe he'll reassure you," said Ma. "And in any case, he's the person Avril needs to see if she's going to sign up. Why don't you drive her there tomorrow. If you're still unhappy after talking to Perce, you can bring her straight home again."

Avril kicked the wall. What if Fa wasn't convinced by Perce? Ma hadn't exactly won the battle for her!

As they drove along Main Street, Avril couldn't help looking for Sam, hoping to see him even though she knew he'd be in school. They were soon at Mr Trigg's house and pulled up alongside his Square. In the far corner, a couple of people were stooped over the ground, planting.

Fa climbed the porch steps and knocked. They waited a few minutes and were about to knock again when the door opened slowly.

"Hello, hello," said Mr Trigg. "Josh Fairburn, isn't it?"

"Yes," said Fa curtly.

"And this is?"

"Avril, my youngest."

"Nice to meet you, Avril," beamed Mr Trigg.

"Hi, Mr Trigg."

"Call me Perce. How can I help?"

"I was hoping to speak with you," said Fa, "about

the Community Growing Scheme, among other things."

"Ah! Marvellous! Come in, come in!"

They followed Perce slowly along the corridor and hovered while he eased himself into a recliner.

"Sit down, please!" he said, the chair whirring as he used the remote to adjust its height and leg rest. "What can I do for you?"

"I want to volunteer–"

"Hang on, hang on!" Fa cut her off brusquely.

"What? You said I could!"

Fa raised his hand and Avril recognised the gesture. It was the one that always shut the family up. She subsided, and looked at Perce who gave her a quick sympathetic smile. He turned his attention to Fa and waited. The expectant silence seemed to unsettle Fa and his face reddened a little.

"I... I need to know more about the scheme. And about the town and the sort of people who've signed up."

"What do you want to know?" Mr Trigg cocked his head on one side, seeming to examine Fa.

"Who's doing it? Who makes the decisions? Who's in charge? How do you decide who's in charge? How long will it go on for – what's the long-term plan? What sort of people are involved? Are they trustworthy?"

"That's a lot of questions," Perce observed gently.

Fa opened his mouth to say more, but Perce stopped him with a raised hand.

"I'll try to answer them. So, first, let me see…" He thought for a second, tapping his forefinger on his knee. "No-one's in charge. I manage the schedule, but I don't tell anyone what to do. Everyone chooses their tasks when they volunteer. It's evolving. We don't really know how it will work yet."

Perce leaned forward in his chair, his gaze intense. "You were at the meeting. You know it's just a shambolic mess of people having a go at something new. I think there's just one question you really want me to answer: Can you trust us?"

Fa went even redder but held Perce's stare. "Well, can we?"

Avril held her breath, hoping for the right answer, the statement that would convince Fa everything was fine and of course he should let her join the scheme.

"I don't know."

Avril's exhalation was anguished. Perce glanced at her and gave her a mysterious nod, perhaps intended as reassurance.

"Listen, Josh – can I call you Josh?"

Fa's nod was impatient.

"Listen, I can't claim to like and trust every single person in this town. Some of them are ratbags. Same as anywhere. But most of them aren't. Most of them are ordinary, nice people."

"Most."

"Yes!" Perce seemed to search for words, then spoke softly. "Listen, I know your farm suffered at the hands of strangers some time ago–"

"How do you know that?" Fa's voice was harsh.

"Your lovely daughter Natasha is also a lovely chatterbox."

Perce smiled, and Avril could imagine Natasha monologuing at him in her excitable way.

"So I understand why you might be suspicious."

"Can you swear to me the raiders weren't people from town?"

Fa's question was like a knife dropped onto a wooden floor, standing upright on its sharp tip and quivering in the silence.

Perce shook his head slowly. "I can't swear."

Fa stared at him.

Perce continued, his voice steady. "I don't think it was anyone from Newbeck. More likely gangs from the city – remember the unrest? We didn't have riots here. We didn't have much more than a bit of graffiti."

Perce took a deep breath. "I can't swear because I don't know. But that isn't the point."

"What is the point?"

"You have to take a chance on people. Start from the assumption that they're decent. Because most likely they are, even if a few of them are ratbags. And treating them like they're decent makes them more likely to be decent."

Avril couldn't tell what Fa was thinking. His face was unmoving.

Then he dropped another question. "Would you ever steal food?"

"No," Perce replied, "I wouldn't take what's not mine. And I've been hungry every day that I can remember." He thought for a moment. "But..." he added.

Fa jumped into the pause. "But what?"

"Would you? If your children were actually starving?"

Neither of them spoke. Avril waited. Fa rubbed his head. Perce tapped his knee.

"Like I was saying, you can't wait for everyone and everything to be perfect before you take a chance. Good enough has to be good enough, or we'd never do anything."

Avril nodded, her eyes on Fa's unreadable expression.

"Lots of people in town haven't signed up for the scheme," said Perce. "There's a risk that we plant apple trees and people who didn't contribute nick the apples. But equally they might see our harvests and decide to join in. You can't predict, you just have to take the chance. And one thing I can swear to, is that the scheme is already transforming Newbeck."

"How?" Avril dared to whisper.

"So many ways!" Perce's walnut face shone. "Neighbours talking to each other! People working together with a sense of possibility! You can see them changing."

"How?" Avril nudged, watching Fa's unchanging face for a reaction.

"Give you an example. Couple of ruffian kids about your age. Well-off but neglected, so they're brimful of entitlement and anger. Twins, and they've formed a two-person gang against the world."

"Oh, I think I've seen them," Avril remembered the boys teasing Sam.

"Well, I was watching them planting out some seedlings with your sister the other day. And they looked different. Calm. I'd never seen them like that. Because I think – and this is just my theory – I think... it's impossible to sustain fury when you're putting your whole attention onto a plant. When you're really looking at nature, you just can't stay angry."

Perce flapped a hand apologetically. "I know, I'm a sentimental, silly old man! Anyway, you can't deny the physical changes in town – they're everywhere. Wild grasses and flowers beautifying the verges! Different seedlings on different Squares. Even my windowsill. Look!"

Avril went over to the window and looked at the narrow tray of soil; a row of plants stretched small leaves towards the sunshine.

"Nice selection," she said, lightly touching them. "Chard, kale, mizuna, rocket."

"Known by me as 'salad'," said Perce, looking delighted. "Your brother Ben told me I should be eating more greens. 'Get your strength up,' he says. Funny boy! He and Natasha brought me these and I've been having a few leaves every day."

Avril's imploring eyes met Fa's. It was awful that Perce could be so excited by the pathetic assortment of plants. Fa had to be thinking the same thing.

Fa stood up and came over to the window, but instead of looking at the plants, he stared outside at the empty Square. Avril felt his hand heavy on her shoulder.

"Looks like you need an irrigation system out there," said Fa. "Avril could make a start on that now if you like?"

Avril saw her smile reflected on Perce's face.

"That would be marvellous," he said.

"I'd like to look at the planting schedule," said Fa. "Might have some suggestions."

Avril went outside and took string, a measuring tape and notebook from the pockets of her dungarees. The two people working on Perce's Square turned out to be Sam's neighbour, Bridget, and her partner, Rose. They had just finished planting squash and courgette seeds in neat rows, and were happy to help Avril measure the area before they left.

Avril checked the distance to the waterbutts at the side of the house and began sketching a rough diagram in her notebook. She was perched on the top porch step when the door opened. It was Perce.

"I'm making a pot of tea for me and your dad," he said. "Would you like some?"

Avril was about to answer, when a sixth sense made her look up the street. There, at the far end, were two bicycles, approaching fast.

Sam and Casey were wheeling towards her. Casey was sitting upright, confidently cycling hands-free and talking animatedly. Sam was crouched over the handlebar cycling alongside his brother and staring straight ahead. They drew closer. Avril gripped the notebook. It didn't seem like Sam was going to see her, but at the last minute, as he whizzed past, he glanced sideways. Avril saw his eyes widen with recognition, but he didn't wave or smile. She jumped to her feet and watched as the bicycles hurtled along the street. Sam turned his head and looked at her, then they disappeared round the corner. Avril's heart was pulsing like a finger jammed in a hinge.

"Avril?"

Perce was leaning on his sticks in the doorframe, waiting. She felt him looking at her.

"Tea?"

Avril managed to speak. "Sure. Thanks."

"Would you give me a hand in the kitchen?" he said. "I don't normally make a pot. It might be too heavy for me."

They walked past the living room, where Josh was sitting at the table poring over a file of papers. In the kitchen, Perce directed Avril to the tea caddy and got her to pour the boiled water into the teapot.

"Give it a minute to brew," he said, then went on quietly. "So. Those boys. Why did they make you look like you'd been slapped by the ghost of an ancestor?"

Avril wondered if she could get away with a lie.

"Sorry to be nosy," said Perce. "I just don't like seeing people upset."

She decided on a half-truth. "The older one. I thought he was a friend. But we had an argument. He said I was moaning and selfish."

"Ah." Perce looked thoughtful. "Sorry to hear that."

"So I felt uncomfortable seeing him."

Even as she spoke the words, Avril knew she'd lied. She felt uncomfortable not seeing him. She wasn't upset by his presence. She was upset because he hadn't stopped. Her heart was still calming down after just glimpsing him pass by. She wanted to see Sam, and embrace him, and explain, and apologise, and for him to apologise, too; she wanted to talk with him, and she wanted to kiss him. She focused on the thin wisp of steam emerging from the teapot spout, trying to stop her brain swirling. She could feel Perce watching her.

"D'you think the tea's ready?" she said, trying to sound normal.

"I'm sure it is," said Perce. "Let's take it through."

Avril picked up the tray.

"Try not to let stupid comments by stupid boys get to you," he said, his old face rumpling in a warm smile. "You're worth ten of them."

Avril wanted to cry. That was just the problem. She wasn't worth ten of him. Sam was right. She was a selfish moaning horrible person.

THIRTEEN

Sam

It had been three weeks. More than three weeks: three weeks and four days since the argument. Sam couldn't stop thinking about Avril.

He'd been counting on seeing her at the Community Meeting. When that hope was dashed, Sam had started attending as many growth workshops as possible in the hope of seeing her. He'd learnt from Natasha about transplanting seedlings – even braving the presence of the twins who'd been weirdly quiet – but Avril hadn't been there. He'd learnt about pruning from Ben, and discovered that Avril's brother was really funny, but Avril hadn't been there. He'd even bunked off school one morning to see if Avril was at Dustin's propagation workshop; she wasn't, and Sam had been forced to beat a hasty retreat when he spotted Clifford, the school caretaker, taking part.

He was starting to wonder if she was locked up in the valley. Maybe her parents weren't ever going to let her come to town again.

And then he saw her. Cycling home from school with Casey, he'd been thinking about the cave-tunnels to the valley and whether he dared try to navigate them on his own, when he looked up and there she was. Sitting casually on Mr Trigg's porch as if she lived there. She'd stared at him and he'd cycled straight past.

Sam was still kicking himself. He and Casey had been rushing home from school. He'd been so surprised to see Avril that it had taken him a minute to process the fact that she was really there, and to realise he could stop and talk to her. He'd already rounded the corner at the end of the street when he screeched to halt and left a confused Casey waiting by the road as he ran back to Mr Trigg's.

Avril had gone. Sam had almost knocked on the door, but when he recognised the electric farm vehicle parked outside, he realised one or both of her parents must be inside with her and lost his nerve. Josh hated him and Sophie probably wouldn't welcome his presence. But Sam had regretted not knocking ever since.

At last, it was the weekend and now here he was, standing on Mr Trigg's porch, hoping against hope that Avril might be inside.

Sam rapped hard on the door for a third time. He couldn't believe no-one was in.

A voice floated from inside. "I'm coming, I'm coming! Have patience!"

After a couple more minutes, Mr Trigg pulled open the front door. "Why are you in such a hurry? House on fire?" The old man wore such a stern expression that Sam felt quite sheepish.

"Sorry."

"It takes me a bit longer to get around, now I'm not so young and spry," said Mr Trigg, making the word spry sound like an accusation.

"Sorry, I just–"

"So you youngsters need to learn to wait and have a bit of empathy for those of us with physical challenges!" Mr Trigg glared.

Sam had the strong feeling that, for some reason – not just his urgent door-knocking – the man didn't like him. There was an awkward silence. Sam knew with disappointed certainty that Avril wasn't inside.

Mr Trigg leaned on his sticks and peered sideways at him. "What do you want?"

"Er..." Sam struggled to improvise in the face of such hostility. "Er, well, I was hoping you could let me see the community tasks schedule for next week?"

"Why?"

"Um, because... because I was hoping to swap shifts with someone?"

Belatedly, Sam sensed that presenting his excuse as a question was unlikely to sound convincing.

"Really?"

"Because... Because..."

"Yes?"

"Because I need to see Avril!" Sam blurted the truth.

"Oh?" Mr Trigg's eyes became even beadier. "Why?"

"I need to talk to her."

"Why?"

Sam felt like his entrails were being twanged.

"Can't you just let me see the timetable?"

"No."

"Why not?"

"Because she doesn't want to see you."

"She – what? She's talked to you? What did she say? Tell me! Please!"

"Why should I tell you?"

Sam hesitated, feeling desperate. "She's mad at me. And I need to say sorry."

Mr Trigg pursed his lips and looked appraisingly at Sam. "I don't like standing around. My legs ache. Come into the kitchen and tell me your side of the story."

"Okay," said Sam, his innards still feeling jangled.

He followed Mr Trigg slowly into the house.

"... So, you see Mr Trigg, I really need to speak to her," Sam concluded five minutes later, watching the old man's face for signs of sympathy.

He drummed his fingers on the kitchen table in the silence that followed, hoping he'd won Mr Trigg over with his honest account.

"Hmm," said Mr Trigg. "Hmm." He pinched his lower lip, thoughtfully between finger and thumb, then released it. "Call me Perce."

Sam waited. First-name terms seemed like a good sign, but Perce still hadn't said anything about Avril.

"You hurt her," said Perce, wearing his stern expression.

The memory of the argument flared up and Sam nodded, his face burning.

"She told me she thought you were friends. That you'd said nasty things to her," Perce continued. "And that she felt uncomfortable seeing you. So I can't let you see the schedule. If I told you where to find her, I'd be betraying her trust."

Sam's hopes dissolved and he stared at his hands. His fingers stopped drumming.

"But it sounds to me like you were both partly to blame," said Perce. "And that all this might just be a misunderstanding. So..."

Sam looked up.

"... I could give her a message, if you like."

"Yes! Please!"

"Alright then. What do you want me to say?"

FOURTEEN

Avril

Avril levered the nail with her claw-hammer and extracted it in one smooth movement. She dropped it into the tin bucket and gripped the plank with her other hand. One more nail to go and the section was done.

She wanted to preserve as much of the fence for reuse as possible. The wood was strong and the nails could be used again provided they weren't bent out of shape. Any misshapen ones would go to Denley Emmett for his latest art project – he was welding hundreds of small pieces of metal into a giant abstract sculpture. It was supposed to represent a wild plant, which sounded good, but Avril wished he'd accept her offer of a lesson in blow-torch technique.

It was frustrating that town adults always assumed they knew better than younger people. The valley might be suffocating, but everyone did listen to each other. And things had been better at home since Fa had come round – he'd even given back Avril's bike, so she could cycle to town for her community tasks.

Avril had been working to dismantle the fence all morning. Newbeck had decided to open up sections of the dull manicured park to create rewilded areas for biodiversity, and Avril had been given the job of removing unnecessary boundaries. The work was a bit repetitive, but normally she didn't mind that sort of thing – it left her brain free to plan construction projects or travel itineraries. The problem was getting her mind to focus on proper daydreams rather than him.

Ever since the kiss at the waterhole, Avril had thought about Sam constantly. She hadn't even realised how much he'd filled her head until the thoughts had become negative. Before, the idea of Sam had been a delicious secret, something to hug tight to herself when the family were being annoying, to peep at like a present hidden in the bottom of a wardrobe. Now every time his face popped into her mind, she felt the double stab of guilt and anger. Guilt at her own self-absorbed callousness. Anger at his total lack of understanding. She felt depressed as a wilted plant.

Avril positioned the hammer on the last nail and wrenched it out. Another one for the bucket, and the plank was undamaged too. She laid it on the pile and clasped the fence pole with both gloved hands, jiggling the post to loosen it from the ground.

"Avril!"

Perce was trundling towards her on his mobility scooter.

"Ahoy there!"

He wheeled to a halt a short distance away. Avril could see that his vehicle wouldn't cope with the uneven ground that separated them, so she picked her way across the flower border and met him on the flat path.

"Hello, Perce. How's the irrigation system?"

"Perfect!" he said. "But I'm not here about that. I have something for you."

In the basket of the mobility scooter sat an ear-band, its green charge light winking at her.

"Um…" Avril was confused. "That's really nice of you, Perce, but–"

"That isn't the gift," he interrupted, confusing her even more. "The earband belongs to someone else. I've just borrowed it to lend it to you."

"Right…?" She was beginning to wonder if he was senile.

"You need to listen to what's on it."

"Listen?"

"All will become clear!"

Perce's wrinkle-cracked face was beaming so hugely that Avril decided to humour him.

"Okay, I'll listen." She looked around at the deserted park and half-dismantled fence. "Now?"

He nodded.

Avril lifted the earband from the basket and put it over her head. Immediately, rippling guitar music began pouring into her ears.

She stood still. Was it...?

Sam's voice joined the melody. It felt like he was standing at her side, singing just for her. And as the lyrics continued, she realised he was singing just to her. It was a song about her that only she would understand.

Waterfall girl,
Dirigible dreaming,
Longing for freedom,
Yearning to fly...

When the song finished, Avril's cheeks were wet. She rubbed her face with her sleeve and took off the earband.

Perce was staring tactfully into the distance, as if fascinated by the park's identical rows of ash trees. Questions swelled and floated in Avril's brain like hot air balloons.

She tried to speak. "Did he – what did Sam–?"

"I'm just the messenger." Perce chuckled to himself. She wasn't sure, but he might have added, "Cupid on wheels!"

She could feel herself blushing.

"I – I'd better get on with my tasks," she stammered. "Don't want to get behind... put the rota out of sync."

"Never mind the rota!" said Perce. "The question is, what's your reply?"

Avril didn't know what to say. The park stretched around them, with its sterile lawns and repetitive flowerbeds, the sky empty and blue overhead. She'd become so used to thinking of Sam with pain that she didn't know how to adjust.

"Can I borrow the earband?"

"Of course," said Perce. "Maybe if you see him, you can return it in person."

"It's Sam's?"

Perce nodded.

Avril looked down at the object in her hands, and it was as if she could see Sam's fingers holding it, handing it to her.

"Alright," she decided. "Tell him to meet me at the waterhole. Saturday morning, nine o'clock."

FIFTEEN

Sam

Sam's heart was hammering like an angry percussionist. He'd never cycled so fast in his life. He'd been caught trying to sneak out of the house and almost felt like crying with frustration. How could his parents be so cruel? How could they insist he finish morning chores on a day like this?

What if she doesn't wait?

He forced his legs to work harder, churning up dust as he pedalled wildly along the desert road. The waterhole was in sight. For a moment, it seemed as if the place was deserted and his heart's rhythm juddered.

Then he saw her. She was by the bushes, stooping to retrieve her bike.

"Avril!" he yelled, braking too hard and skidding to a halt.

He jumped off the bike, abandoning it on the dry earth, and ran towards her. Avril straightened up and turned to face him. Sam stopped a couple of metres away from her, awash with anxiety. She looked at him, her face expressionless. He hadn't a clue what she was thinking. His chest heaved, lungs snatching at breath.

"Sorry... for being late," he panted. "My parents..."

He trailed off, intimidated by her cool gaze.

The warm air was full of the sound of the waterfall and tiny birds cheeped in the bushes nearby, but the lack of words made it feel like silence.

Sam's throat was dry. More than anything, he wanted to say the right thing. To get back the feeling of ease there used to be between them. But he could feel his shoulder blades lifting with tension. What if he got it wrong?

Avril's face was unreadable. She didn't look happy, but he couldn't tell if her face was signalling reproach or anxiety. Sam took a step towards her and opened his mouth.

"Wait!" she said.

She let her rucksack slide to the ground and crouched down to open it.

"I brought you..." She rummaged inside. "I hope..."

Standing up again, she held out a small package

but still seemed unable to finish a sentence.

"Um, it's... Here, take it."

Sam walked towards her and reached out to take the package in both hands. They were an arm's length from each other, and he could feel her solemn expression mirrored in his own. He unwrapped the piece of cloth. Inside was a bag of dried apple rings, and a slab of something sticky that looked to contain grains, nuts and seeds.

"I don't want you to be hungry!" Avril blurted, in a voice that held tears. "I'm so sorry!"

"No, I'm sorry!" said Sam quickly. "I shouldn't have – I shouldn't have said those things."

"But you were right! I've never been hungry, except the year of the raid."

"But it's still true that you were trapped in the valley. You were so frustrated you ran away! I forgot. I forgot how you felt."

He didn't know who moved first, but the next second their arms were around each other, hugging each other hard. Avril was the first to break apart, and when she looked at him, Sam was horrified to see the shimmer of a tear on her lower eyelash. He grasped both her hands.

"What is it?" he asked.

"I thought you'd hate me," she said, her voice a little wobbly. "I've never had a friend. I've always been surrounded by family. I've tagged along with older siblings or cousins, but I've never known

other people. So, when I thought you didn't like
me anymore–"

"I could never hate you!"

Sam put his arms around her and held tight, feeling her hair tickling his cheek, her back moving
with her breath. After a second, her arms returned
the pressure, and they held onto each other for a
long moment.

When they broke apart and looked into each
other's faces, it felt like something had shifted
between them.

"I love the song," Avril said quietly.

Sam squeezed her hand, feeling happy for the first
time in weeks. He remembered the food parcel in
his other hand.

"You want to share this?" he said.

"I know," said Avril, "let's climb! There's a ledge
above the waterfall with the best view in the world!"

"Okay," Sam grinned. "Show me!"

Ten minutes later, they were clinging to the rock
face, and beads of sweat were travelling down Sam's
spine. He tried to follow exactly where Avril placed
her hands and feet, but it wasn't as easy as she made
it look.

"Just a little higher!" Avril called.

"Does this mythical ledge exist?" Sam shouted up.

"Or are you luring me to my death in the absence of witnesses?"

"Here!"

He watched her stretch a sneakered foot sideways and made a mental note of where the foothold was. She stepped onto a wide, rocky shelf that was almost invisible from below. Sam climbed the last couple of metres and crawled onto the ledge beside her, Avril shuffling along to make space. Sam cautiously revolved his body to face the right way and sat beside her, shoulder to shoulder, legs dangling. He pulled the package from his pocket and offered Avril an apple ring.

"Thanks," she said, taking one. "You have the rest. And try Auntie Jodi's flapjack. They're really good."

The sky was cornflower blue. From the ledge above the waterfall, they could see the desert road and Newbeck town spread out in miniature. Directly beneath them, the pool churned as water poured into it, ripples spreading to stillness at the edges, where the water was placid and fringed with vegetation.

"There's some seedlings in my rucksack, too," said Avril after a minute. "Pretty much a tradition now, right? That when I see you, I bring random plants!"

Sam grinned and nodded, his mouth full of flapjack.

"I still can't believe my dad has relaxed about letting the family come to town," Avril went on. "I kind of suspect aliens must've abducted Fa and replaced him with a double."

"Yeah, it is pretty amazing," said Sam, remembering how Josh had reacted to his intrusion all those weeks ago.

"He's even let the whole family go to the Summer Fair in the next town today," said Avril. "It's why I figured we might finally get to be alone."

"That's where my parents and Casey are – I think everyone's there."

Sam had a sudden thought. "Did you want to go? You must've missed stuff like that in the valley."

"No." Avril glanced sideways at him and smiled. "I mean, I did hate missing out – when Fa didn't let us go to the Country Show at Easter, I started work on the bike to get me to town. But today... No. Rather be here."

Sam wiped a sweaty hand surreptitiously on his shorts. As if their minds were linked, a second later he felt Avril's fingers twining with his. They leaned against each other and looked out at the view.

"Can't believe it's less than a month since the community scheme started," said Sam. "So much has changed."

"Town does seem different," said Avril. "Busier."

"To be honest," said Sam, "there's been times this month I've regretted the big task-sharing idea."

Avril turned to look at him. "D'you mean–? It was your idea?"

Sam felt embarrassed. "Oh, yeah. Well, it sort of occurred to me. So, I – er, I suggested it to my dad. At the meeting. And we went with it."

"And it's brilliant!" said Avril, beaming.

"It seems to have caused everyone a gazillion times more work."

"Don't be silly. It doesn't feel like work when you're doing something you like! I get to do construction and tech projects instead of weeding, which is a win. Especially now I've got the bike back, and I can come to town more. Breathe the air outside Home Valley! I think the community scheme is fantastic!"

"Yeah, I guess so."

Sam hadn't really thought about how the new system was affecting people's lives. He'd been too busy worrying about how he'd screwed things up with Avril. He felt heartened by her positivity.

"What do you think about the new town currency idea?"

"The NewBuck! Such a great name!" said Avril.

"That meeting nearly killed me – all the endless debate about the system of credits, and how we measure if different tasks are worth the same!"

"I'm glad they went with NewBucks. It's so cool having your own money."

"Or it will be, once they get it up and running! In the meantime it's an–"

"Administrative Nightmare!" Avril chorused with him. "Poor Perce."

"He loves it!"

"True," she agreed. "He might complain–"

"Constantly!"

"– constantly! But he's absolutely buzzing."

"Anyway," said Sam, running his thumb over her rough knuckles, "I'm just glad everyone's distracted today."

"Oh no!" Avril exclaimed, her voice suddenly full of dread.

"What's wrong?"

"Look!"

SIXTEEN

Avril

Far away on the desert horizon, a puff of dust trailed behind a line of small black beads.

"AgriCarriers," whispered Avril. "And they're heading for town."

Sam looked as petrified as she felt.

"No-one's there to stop them. They'll rip up the new planting." Avril's heart was like a fist hammering on a door. "We have to warn everyone."

"My comscreen's in my rucksack," said Sam, "with the bikes. Let's climb down."

"No time!" said Avril. "Let's jump."

Sam's eyes widened. "You serious?"

"Of course." Avril met his gaze. "We can't waste a minute. Don't worry, the pool's deep enough. It's safe. I've done it before."

She didn't add that, although her older siblings regularly made the jump, she'd only done it once, last summer when Ben's taunting had become unbearable. Instead, she got to her feet carefully and stood on the rim of the ledge. Sam stood beside her and gripped her hand; the warm, firm hold gave her courage.

"Don't think," she said. "On three."

They counted together: "One – Two – Three–"

On the final count, they bent their legs and launched themselves into the air. It was only a few seconds, but to Avril it felt like flying, as if time had stopped for a momentary breath. A fractional hover in mid-air, then they plunged down into the heart of the pool, beyond the churning waterfall froth, where the water was deepest and coldest. The icy shock was like having the oxygen slapped from her lungs, and Avril immediately kicked hard to regain the surface. She shook wet hair from her eyes like a dog and Sam bobbed up alongside her, both gasping warm summer air as if they'd been holding their breath for minutes rather than seconds.

"Come on!" Sam swam quickly to the edge and ran to where the bikes lay waiting for them. He pulled out his comscreen and was already speaking as Avril made her way through the water. Townids probably got more swimming practice, she reflected as she doggy-paddled to land.

"My parents just had a warning from the roadcam

monitor," said Sam, putting his comscreen away and extending a hand to help her out. "Everyone's coming. But they won't make it back before the AgriCarriers reach town. We have to–"

"– get there first." Avril completed his sentence, shivering, and without saying anything more they grabbed their bags and bikes and headed for town as fast as they could.

Water was squeezing out of Avril's sneaker soles with every press of the pedals, and her clothes dripped a wet trail as they cycled. At first, she was quivering with cold, but their hectic pace meant she soon warmed up, even though her wet garments were clammy and cool on her skin. Sam was a little ahead of her. Looking past him, she could see the GreenCult convoy getting closer by the minute. The vehicles hadn't yet reached the desert road; there was still a chance they could beat them to town.

Avril's legs and lungs were burning. She could hear Sam breathing hard, too. Her skin had dried completely – only her clothes and hair were still wet.

"Come on! Come on!"

She wasn't sure why Sam was wasting his breath on words, then understood he was trying to keep himself going – to keep them both going.

"We're nearly there!" she gasped. "We can do it!"

"Yeah," Sam panted, "Come on! Come on!"

They were nearly at the edge of town, at the end of Sam's street. His house was the first. His Square would be the first to be destroyed. Her heart twisted like a knot being pulled tight. She couldn't bear to watch them smash it to pieces again. She glanced over her shoulder – the convoy was turning onto the road behind them. Guards in black stood on running boards on the sides of the AgriCarriers, like rows of toy soldiers. Each was gripping a truncheon.

Avril and Sam skidded to a halt. They'd made it. They'd beaten the convoy to town.

They looked at each other.

"What do we do?" whispered Avril. "How do we stop them?"

Sam shook his head, desperate and unsure.

"We block the road?" said Avril, scrabbling for ideas.

"Yes! But with what? Nothing's big enough."

"With ourselves?"

They laid their bicycles across the street, and stood between them, in the middle of the road, holding hands.

The convoy came closer.

"They won't run us down," said Avril.

"They can't," said Sam. He sounded as uncertain as the tremble in her voice.

The first vehicle was a hundred metres away. The guards hanging off either side started shouting and waving their arms, ordering them out of their path. Avril gripped Sam's hand harder, not caring that both their palms were slick with sweat. He glanced at her and his face was rigid.

"Get off the road!"

"Get out of the way!"

"We will run you down!"

"They won't," whispered Avril, trying to convince herself. "They won't."

"MOVE!" yelled a guard. "MOVE!"

"They won't," she said again.

"GET OFF THE ROAD!"

"MOVE!"

The AgriCarrier was still approaching. Avril felt Sam's hand gripping hers so hard it almost hurt. An acrid metallic smell emanated from the vehicle. There was the black flash of a shiny truncheon in the air. She started to feel dizzy. The vehicle was nearly on them.

And then –

It stopped.

Sam's arm went around Avril's shoulders. They stood firm, side by side.

"Oi, you two. Get out the way!" A guard had jumped down and was strutting towards them. "We've had reports of illegal planting. We're here to remove the unauthorised soil and crops."

"We're not moving," Sam said, his voice calm, although Avril could swear she felt a tremor in his body.

"Move it!"

More guards were approaching.

"You're obstructing our lawful and necessary actions."

Avril stuck her chin out. "We're not moving."

"You need. To get out. Of our way."

The first guard spoke very slowly, as if they were imbeciles.

"We are. Not moving. Today."

Avril mimicked him, then felt a flash of fear as his truncheon flew into the air.

"See this?" He paused, with the weapon aloft. "This really hurts. When it hits you."

"You can't," said Sam. "That's illegal."

The guard leaned towards them and Avril flinched.

"You see any police here?" he said. "Any witnesses? Oh yeah, that's right. About fifty witnesses. On these trucks. Who'll all agree with me."

The guards who were gathering in the road laughed in agreement.

"SO MOVE!"

The guards lined up, some of them smacking truncheons into the palm of their hands or practising swinging their weapons. Avril couldn't help imagining how much it would hurt to be struck. Bones would break.

She looked at Sam.

"I don't know," he whispered.

Avril swallowed. She was about to speak – though what the words would be she didn't know – when they were interrupted by a humming noise.

Brrrrrrrrrrrr.

She looked at the guards; they were watching something on the road behind her. Without moving her feet, Avril looked over her shoulder and saw where the sound was coming from.

Brrrrrrrrrrrrrrrrrr.

Perce was driving his mobility scooter at the top of its range, and the motor was quietly screaming in complaint. His walking sticks stuck out haphazardly on either side, making the tiny vehicle look like it had legs as well as wheels.

"STOP!" Perce yelled. "STOP!"

He slammed on the brakes too late, and Avril and Sam had to jump apart as he hurtled between them. Perce parked the mobility scooter at a random angle in front of them. The guards backed away, watching as he laboriously began to lever himself out of the seat. Sam went to help him, but Perce shouted him away.

"Stay there! Hold position! I'm coming!"

A long minute later, Perce stood in the middle of the road, propped up on his sticks like a leggy insect, with Sam's and Avril's hands on his elbows for extra support.

"We shall not be moved!" he announced grandly.

The guards had clustered at the nearest Green-Cult vehicle and were discussing the situation in urgent mutters.

Avril strained her ears to hear what they were saying but only caught a few phrases.

"... that old man... just a couple of kids... drag them... Yeah, but it'll look... and he's disabled..."

"How did you know to come?" Sam asked Perce.

"Clifford, the caretaker. He was monitoring the road cameras. Saw dust in the distance. Knew I was home. Most people are at the fair."

"Why didn't Clifford come with you?"

"He's gone to get weapons from the school broom cupboard. Eccentric, that's what he is."

Avril caught Sam's eye and raised an eyebrow.

Sam smiled briefly then fixed his gaze back on the guards. They were arguing now, disagreeing about how to tackle the situation. The leader was gesticulating with his truncheon, and it was disturbingly obvious how he wanted to deal with things. At least half the group were in opposition, but his voice was loudest.

Avril crossed her fingers.

"Here I am!" Clifford screeched to a halt behind them and added his bike to the blockade.

"Brooms!" he said emphatically, handing them one each.

"Weapons?" said Perce.

"Symbolic! Non-violent action, mate!"

"Oh."

Avril couldn't tell if Perce was disappointed or approving.

"And I brought you a folding chair."

Clifford opened up a striped picnic chair. This

time, it was easy to see that Perce was genuinely relieved.

"Thank you!" said Perce. "That's terribly kind."

Watching Clifford place the chair carefully behind Perce, Avril wondered where the caretaker's fearsome reputation came from – he didn't seem remotely scary today. Then she remembered him volunteering for night shifts. Perhaps his fabled grumpiness at school was just a side-effect of his insomnia.

"We got complacent," said Clifford in dire tones, helping Perce sit down. "Shouldn't have left town unprotected."

"Very true," Perce said.

"People have started to talk in other towns," Clifford said sagely. "Word is spreading that there are other ways to live."

He propped Perce's two walking sticks against the arm of the chair.

"Right," said Clifford, looking around him. "What are we doing?"

"Erm..." said Avril, looking at the bizarre scene: three bicycles, one mobility scooter and four assorted humans with brooms, blocking the way of an immense convoy of AgriCarriers and an army of professional security guards. "We're kind of just... waiting."

"Yeah," Sam agreed.

"Right-y-ho." Clifford seemed unperturbed. "We'll wait."

It felt like hours had passed, although it couldn't have been. The sun hadn't even made it halfway towards its midday height, and Avril's clothes remained faintly damp. The GreenCult guards were still bickering and had gradually drawn more of their colleagues from the back of the convoy into the argument. They seemed to be preparing to take some sort of vote.

Avril was starting to feel tired just from standing still for so long. She and Sam were shoulder to shoulder, holding hands and each gripping an absurd broom in the other hand. Clifford stood on the other side of Perce, who was comfortably ensconced in his chair. The school caretaker held his broom with the stance of a Trojan warrior, while Perce clasped a mop on his lap like a knight ready to joust.

"Look," Sam whispered into Avril's ear.

In the distance, hurtling along the road, was another convoy – a motley race pack of all the vehicles in town. Electrics led the way, including two small delivery vans from the Library of Things, the school minibus, a couple of farm vehicles that Avril recognised as belonging to her family, and the little fleet of local taxis. They were followed by a horde of cyclists going hell for leather. The members of the Community Growing Scheme had all abandoned the summer fair and were sprinting back to Newbeck in a straggling mass.

As soon as the guards noticed the approaching crowd, it triggered further, even more heated arguments.

Avril squeezed Sam's hand and felt the relief in his responding pressure.

As the gaggle grew closer, Avril could see that some of the vehicles were able to travel much faster than others. The cyclists were some way behind, and the tractor was trundling almost as slowly near the back of the group. The first vehicle to reach them was the farm quad bike, driven at unprecedented speed by Fa, Sam's dad riding pillion behind him. Without a pause, Fa swung it in a circle and bounced to a stop alongside the blockade.

The two adults dismounted and ran towards them. Sam and Avril let go of each other's hands and moved apart a little. Avril was surprised when Fa enveloped her in a huge hug.

"Are you alright?" he asked, still holding her tight.

"Yes," said Avril, feeling inexplicably tearful. She firmed up her voice. "Yes, we're fine."

"Are you okay?" Sam's dad asked.

"Yes," said Sam, allowing him a similar hug.

Perce's quavering voice called across from his chair.

"I'm fine, thank you!"

Avril laughed, and Fa went to shake his hand. More people were arriving – including Ma and siblings – abandoning vehicles all over the road and running the last bit of the way. The blockade grew bigger. People linked arms, forming a human chain.

"LISTEN TO ME!"

It was the leader of the GreenCult squad. Everyone turned to look at him.

"CLEAR THE ROAD!"

"No!" called Perce, in his reedy voice.

At that moment, a swarm of cyclists whizzed down the street, skidding and braking, jumping off and adding their bicycles to the blockade. Then they ran, panting and smiling, to link arms with the others.

"ATTENTION!"

The guards fell into formation. The two groups faced each other, the uniformed guards in stern rows, the civilians a messy, colourful line.

The head guard walked forwards and faced the lines of townspeople. He addressed Fa, who was standing in the centre between Perce and Avril.

"You! Tell them to clear the road!"

Fa laughed in his face.

"Fine," said the head guard, his voice full of menace. "We'll be back. You hear? WE'LL BE BACK!"

He turned on his heel and stomped towards the convoy.

"Wait!" Avril broke free of the chain and picked up her rucksack. She took out a strawberry plant and ran to the guard. "Here."

The man turned and looked at her.

"This is what we're trying to grow. You can have it. You could grow strawberries too."

He knocked the plant from her hand.

With a shout of fury, Fa ran forward and Avril grabbed him around the waist to stop him punching the guard. She could feel Fa's rage like a physical vibration.

"Don't!" she said desperately. "Don't, Fa! I'm fine!"

He stayed still. Locked in place with Fa, Avril stared at the guard. The man stared back at them, and she saw that the anger in his face was mixed with confusion and helplessness. Avril willed him to acknowledge it, to admit he wasn't as certain and violent as he seemed. The man opened his mouth as if to speak, then turned abruptly and walked away. They watched him march along the line of vehicles, his spine rigid within its uniform, and Avril felt a weird combination of sadness and triumph.

"Can I take it?"

Another GreenCult employee, a short, dark-moustached man, had sneaked forward from his post. Avril immediately recognised him as the guard she'd spoken to all those weeks ago, when the AgriCarriers had been delivering seeds and soil.

"Yes," she said.

He picked up the small plant and tucked it quickly into his pocket, then ran back to his place by the nearest AgriCarrier, just in time. The head guard had reached the end of the convoy and shouted his order.

"REVERSE!"

With a swiftness that exposed their relief, the guards resumed travel positions on the running boards, gripping handles on the exterior of the vehicles and standing bolt upright in an attempt to regain their dignity.

Slowly, the line of machines began to reverse.

A hush fell as the people of Newbeck watched the AgriCarriers slink backwards and turn themselves around. The silence held as the convoy rolled away from town. Avril held her breath. The crowd were as still as trees on a calm day.

"WOOO-HOOO!" Sam's brother Casey yelled, and it was like a raincloud releasing a deluge. The quiet shattered, human chains fragmented into in-dividuals, and the air filled with noise. Some of the crowd were cheering and shouting; others talked urgently in groups, faces sombre with the prospect of the AgiCarriers' return.

Avril let go of Fa and looked up at him. "I'm glad you didn't hit him."

He nodded and gripped her shoulder, then they both turned and looked at the buzzing scene. Perce waved his mop at the sky.

"Hip hip HURRAH!"

SEVENTEEN

Sam

The street felt like a party, an orchestra of chatter as people embraced family and neighbours, hugging acquaintances they'd never properly spoken to.

Sam saw Casey dancing and leading classmates in a chant. "We diiiid it we diiiiid it..."

Meanwhile, his parents were at the centre of a huddle of people split between congratulating themselves and earnestly planning future defensive action. Even people who weren't part of the community scheme started to arrive in the road, drawn to find out what all the noise was about.

Sam felt a hefty slap on his shoulder and found Clifford beaming at him.

"Well done, Sam! If you and Avril hadn't got here

when you did, well, don't like to think how much planting we could've lost."

"Thanks," said Sam, smiling back.

Out of the corner of his eye, he saw Caldo and Marley watching as Clifford put up his palm for a high five.

"Glad you came when you did." Sam high-fived him. "We needed you and Perce to hold the road."

"Teamwork!" Clifford said, grinning massively and smacking Sam's shoulder again.

Sam noticed the twins' astonished stares and felt warm inside.

"Put those down!" Clifford suddenly yelled in his scary school voice, and two little kids who'd been sword-fighting with the brooms dropped them and ran away in terror. The twins backed away instinctively.

"Little horrors," said Clifford to Sam, sounding almost benevolent, and strode off to retrieve his symbolic weapons.

Sam sauntered past Marley and Caldo with a casual nod. They both nodded back, still frozen with surprise at his new friendship with the terrifying caretaker. Sam stopped and looked at them.

"She *is* my girlfriend, by the way."

Neither of them spoke for a second, then Marley cleared his throat.

"Oh, er..."

Sam waited.

"Excellent." Caldo filled in the blank.

"Yeah. Yeah, excellent," agreed Marley.

Sam nodded and walked away.

He scanned the crowd but couldn't see Avril anywhere. Maybe her family would know where she was. Her mum and siblings were in the middle of a huge group of people, all talking and laughing. Sam was considering fighting his way through the crowd when a deep voice stopped him.

"Sam."

He stopped. It was Josh.

"Er, yeah?" Sam turned to face him.

"I've just heard that the community scheme was your idea."

Sam wished he knew what Avril's dad was thinking.

"Er, yeah. Yeah, it was."

Josh held out a massive hand. Sam stared at it, not knowing what to do.

"Put it there, Sam."

Josh's face was doing something Sam had never seen before. Was that... a smile? Obediently, he took Josh's hand, and the energetic shake went up his entire arm. With each pumping handshake, Josh fired another awkward nugget of praise.

"Initiative. Good job. And today. Well done."

"Er, thanks. Thank you. Sir."

Josh nodded and released him.

Sam watched him go, then looked around. Where

was she? The street was so full of people, in noisy clusters and gaggles; he couldn't see Avril anywhere. He jogged along the edge of the road, scanning the crowds.

There!

Sam ran over to where she was standing, by his family's Square, and hugged her. Avril hugged him back, then broke away and looked anxiously at the crowd. Sam realised what she was thinking.

"Your dad just spoke to me."

"And?" Avril was hesitant.

"He shook my hand!"

"No!"

"Yes!"

"So we...?"

"I mean, maybe... I think maybe he's okay with us."

Avril raised her eyebrows, then smiled and slid her arm around his waist. Sam responded with an arm around her shoulder and they leaned against each other for a minute, watching the buzzing crowd.

"Avril?" said Sam.

"Mm?"

"Why did you try to give that plant to the worst guard?"

She shrugged. "Spur of the moment thing, I suppose." Then she looked sheepish and said, "Actually, I remembered something Perce said. You can't stay angry when you're really looking at a plant!

Sounds silly now. I guess... I guess I was trying to reach him, the guard. Find a way to get through to him."

She sounded suddenly worried. "Did it look stupid?"

"No!" said Sam. "Not stupid! Kind of brilliant, actually."

They looked sideways at each other. Both moved at the same time, arms lacing around each other, bodies pressing together as they kissed.

The sound of birdsong in the blue sky mingled with the noisy chatter of the gathered people of Newbeck.

When they stopped kissing, Avril pointed to Sam's Square. "You'll have strawberries soon."

Hand in hand, they stood together and looked at the strawberry plants flourishing green against the dark soil.

THE END

If you've enjoyed Dirt, *please help other readers
to find it by writing a brief review on your favourite
book site!*

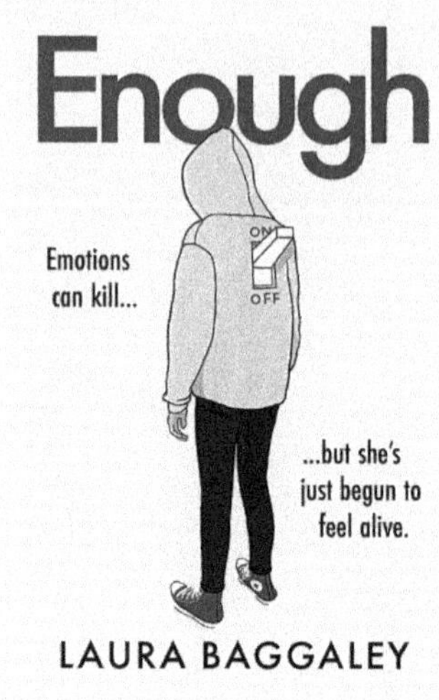

A medical breakthrough solves the problem of endless old age: if a person has had enough of life, their 'Switch' flips and they instantly die.

Fifteen-year-old Margaretta lives in fear of her Switch. Since her mum died four years ago, she has lived alone with her violent father and survived only by shutting out all feelings. Margaretta's emotional armour starts to crack when she meets Sky, a charismatic vagabond, and runs away with him.

Sky introduces Margaretta to the exhilarating atmosphere of the Blue Cat nightclub. But as the attraction between them intensifies, they find themselves drawn into a murky world of political corruption controlled by the club's shady clientele. With dishonesty eating away at the heart of power, countless lives are on the line.

Emotions can kill, but Margaretta has just begun to feel alive.

Sign up to the newsletter for updates about forthcoming books at laurabaggaley.co.uk

ACKNOWLEDGEMENTS

I have loved working on *Dirt*, not because writing it was easy but because I've been able to call on such a wonderful accumulation of people in the making of it.

Stewart – first reader of my first manuscript, and still the first person I go to with a first draft. THANK YOU! Your insights are always spot on and essential, and our conversations over the years have made me a better writer.

Jono – I'm so lucky that my brilliant, lovely brother happens also to be an insightful and astute reader. Thank you for all your thoughts, and for helping unlock a jammed bit of plot.

Alice, Kath and Rachel – fellow genre pioneers! Thank you for reading Dirt with thrutopia in mind, your invaluable comments and always-inspiring conversations. And thanks to the rest of the thrutopian team, Ilse and Hilary, it's a joy working with everyone on *Bending the Arc*.

Huge thanks to the Habitat Press team – Rananda, for all your brilliant manuscript notes (and especially for teaching me about commas), and Denise, for your impeccable suggestions (and for teaching me about compost!).

Sue Copsey, wonderful editor, thank you for your cheerful emails and elegant edits!

Jet Purdie, thank you for the stunning book cover; you are a genius.

Julia, Rishi, Toby and Alice – aka the Invalid Club – thank you for blurb-reading and listening and advising, and for all the happy hours spent comparing injuries.

Katie, Mel, Emma, Hannah, Becki, Rachel Grim and Smiley Rachel – best book group in the world – thank you for unflagging moral support, intelligent bookish conversations and (always) superlative snacks!

Susila, thank you for perfecting the blurb and for ongoing encouragement on all our many walks.

Pauline Wiles, you've supported me as an author right from the start – thank you so much for my beautiful website and all the tips along the way.

Manda Scott, the Thrutopian Masterclass was life-changing. Thank you for leading the way. Heartfelt gratitude to all the speakers on the course and the work they've done and continue to do.

Deep thanks to all the farmers and growers – to the people who feed us and whose work is so often taken for granted. And thank you to those who have shared their ideas and experiences in books and talks and interviews, growers and writers I've never met but who have changed how I think – Guy Watson, Patrick Holden, Mary Reynolds, Matthew Crawford, Caroline Grindod, Iain 'Tolly' Tolhurst, George Monbiot, Michael Pollan and Sarah Langford.

And then my family, left till last because they're the hardest to thank. How to articulate how lucky I feel? EB, thank you for all the books and words from the moment I began. (And for being my 'literary patron'!) Jono (again); bestest brother! Ebba, Godmother extraordinaire, thank you for everything. Michael, my beloved bibliomaniac – thank you for it all (edits and tea and laughs and reminders to breathe and so much more!). Mina and Freya, bringers of joy (and occasionally chaos). All the words in all the books in our flat combined couldn't fully express how much I love you all.

LAURA BAGGALEY is a writer of novels for young adults and theatremaker, and teaches acting and literature at City Lit adult education college in London. Her novel *Enough* was one of three finalists in the Mslexia Children's Novel Competition and was longlisted for the *Times / Chicken House* Children's Fiction Competition. Her second novel, currently in its final draft, was longlisted for the Yeovil Literary Prize. Laura is a firm believer in 'imagination activism' and loves books that ask big questions, usually starting 'What if...?' She enjoys the challenge of creating alternative possible futures in her writing, and hopes that by imagining different worlds we'll be able to build a better one.

Connect with her at laurabaggaley.co.uk